OUT OF PLAY

LOVE IN THE ARENA: BOOK TWO

KAYLA TIRRELL

Copyright © 2020 by Kayla Tirrell

All rights reserved.

No part of this book may be reproduced in any form or by any electronic or mechanical means, including information storage and retrieval systems, without written permission from the author, except for the use of brief quotations in a book review.

This is a work of fiction. Names, characters, businesses, places, locales, and incidents are either the products of the author's imagination or used in a fictitious manner. Any resemblance to actual persons, living or dead, or actual events is purely coincidental.

Proofreading: EditElle

Cover Design: Booked Forever

1

EMMELINE

EMMELINE RUSHED THROUGH THE ARENA, pushing the sleeves of her oversized jersey up her forearms. Thanks to a bitter online bidding war, she'd paid way too much for the top with the name O'Brien on the back, but it had been worth every penny to win the captain's jersey. Not only was it one-of-a-kind—only worn for one game—but all the proceeds went to a local charity. She was happy she got to wear it for the first game she'd been able to attend that season.

Oh, the things you did for your big brother.

Emmeline could hear the crowd going wild as she showed her ticket to the man standing guard at the entrance to the VIP section. She hated being late, and her toe tapped impatiently as she got a wristband that would allow her to go in and out without having to show her ticket every time.

After three years of coming to the games, she'd have thought her brother would have gotten her some special pass rather than dealing with tickets. But no, those were for actual VIPs, and the captain's sister didn't make the cut, apparently.

She rushed past the guard to get to her seat. As Emmeline passed behind the rows of VIP boxes and got closer to the box, she spotted Miriam. The team's community outreach coordinator was cheering loudly from her seat on the floor right next to the Storm's bench.

Emmeline pushed past a few people who were too busy watching the action in front of them to notice her trying to squeeze by. She got to her place just as Miriam pounded on the board separating their seats from the field.

"Let's go, Storm!" Miriam's fierce expression made Emmeline glad she was rooting for the same team.

Despite how scary her friend could be, she always enjoyed watching games with Miriam. They fed off each other's energy and always ended up cheering so loud that they got looks from surrounding fans for being too enthusiastic.

Emmeline cleared her throat. "Hey."

Miriam turned to face Emmeline. Her pale blue eyes widened for the briefest moment before her face broke out into a grin. "Where have you been? I've missed you."

Emmeline smirked. "No you haven't." She tipped her head toward the field, and her red ponytail swayed to the side. She flung it over her shoulder impatiently. "Finn told me you've been pretty occupied with pretty boy out there."

Miriam's cheeks turned pink as Silas, one of the

team's forwards, slowed into a jog just long enough to wink at Miriam.

Emmeline swore she heard a growling noise come from Miriam before she smacked the side of the boards. "Keep your eye on the ball, Jenkins!"

Emmeline giggled. "Just like old times," she said before turning her attention to the game in front of them.

She focused on the guys running back and forth as they battled to get—and keep—possession of the ball. All the while, her brother, Finn, was yelling at them from his place in front of the goal. Bastian, a defender, passed the ball back to Finn. He kicked it down the field. Cardosa, another offensive player, stopped it with a header that went toward the other team's goal. Silas took the shot.

"Goal!" The announcer's voice rang through the arena.

Emmeline looked over at Miriam, expecting to see pride on her face, but her eyes stared blankly into the distance. Emmeline knew that lovey-dovey look and elbowed her in the ribs. "You were so busy daydreaming that you missed your boy get that shot."

Miriam shook her head slightly, and her eyes went to where the players all celebrated in the middle of the field. "It's okay. I'll pull it up online and watch it." She winked at Emmeline. "Just don't tell Silas."

Yeah, right. Like Emmeline had anything to say to Silas. It wasn't that she didn't like him. The guys on the team were all nice enough, but she avoided talking to athletes other than her brother. It was just too painful, on so many levels.

As if he knew Miriam was talking about him, Silas ran over toward the girls.

"Speak of the devil." Emmeline rolled her eyes.

She turned her head away, but not before she caught him kiss Miriam's cheek. It was a gesture Emmeline had seen time and time again. One she hadn't expected to see again after he broke Miriam's heart two years ago, but maybe some people were just meant to be together. And some, like Emmeline, were meant to be alone.

Emmeline turned her attention back to the field as Silas ran back out. The guys were done celebrating their goal, and the ball was back in play. A blond guy she didn't recognize stole the ball from a player on the opposing team and drove it down the field. His footwork was impressive as he managed to dodge two different players trying to steal possession.

She leaned in toward Miriam. "Who's that?"

"You mean Grant?"

Grant. The name didn't ring a bell. "Is Grant the guy with the giant number seven on his jersey passing the ball to Bastian?"

Miriam bumped her shoulder against Emmeline. "You'd know the answer to that if you'd been to any of the games or events this year."

It was true that she hadn't been to any games this season—or watched any online—but it wasn't her fault. She'd been so busy rewriting lesson plans and getting extra certifications that she didn't have a free moment. Besides, she hadn't been completely out of the loop. She'd known about Silas and Miriam, hadn't she? Though that was only because Finn was such a gossipy grandmother when the two of them got together.

Emmeline turned toward Miriam. "Does that mean yes?"

Miriam laughed. "Yes. That's Grant Vaughn. He's a rookie. Graduated from Mercer last year and signed on with the Storm just before the season started."

If he just graduated college in the spring, that meant he was about a year younger than Emmeline. Her gaze wandered to where he stood waiting for gameplay to start again. He pushed his too-long blond hair off his forehead before planting his hands on his hips. His body was lean and toned. He was cute...*very* cute.

She closed her eyes.

Nope. She was not going to let her thoughts go down that road. Grant might be a legit hottie, but so were most of the guys out there. They spent hours training to become finely tuned athletic machines, and somehow lost all common decency in the process. Professional athletes were jerks.

Everyone but her brother, of course.

Emmeline opened her eyes just in time to watch the ref put the ball in front of Grant and blow his whistle. The rookie scanned the field looking for someone to pass the ball to. He found his target and kicked toward Cardosa. Cardosa took the shot...and missed.

The other team kicked it back toward Finn.

Emmeline held her breath as the ball got dangerously close to their goal, and Finn's entire body tensed. He crouched over slightly, ready to dive in either direction to block any shots on him.

Thankfully, another player kicked the ball upfield.

Emmeline released her breath and kept her eyes trained on the game while she tried to catch up with Miriam. "So, how has this season been going?"

"Finn tells you about the drama, not their record?"

Emmeline snorted. "Well, I know their wins and losses. And I know that Finn has had a hard time with Vinny."

Miriam laughed. "Everyone has a hard time with Vinny. They don't call him 'The Box' because he's a peacemaker."

No, they called him that because he spent so much time in the penalty box, the place players went when they were too aggressive on the field. Em still remembered how hard it was to get used to the vastly different rules when Finn started playing arena soccer. Now, she knew them like the back of her hand and had no problem yelling at the refs when they made the wrong call.

"I guess not, but I know it's hard on Finn when his team doesn't gel right. Thankfully, he and Silas kissed and made up."

Miriam turned her head toward Emmeline and lifted her brows. "Oh, I didn't realize there was kissing involved. Should I be jealous?"

Emmeline shook her head. "Shut up. You know what I mean."

"What if Finn's a better kisser than me?"

Emmeline opened her mouth to make a sarcastic

reply, when the ball hit the boards right next to her seat. She yelped and looked up just in time to see Grant and another player sprinting in their direction in a race to get to the ball first. Emmeline barely lifted her arms up before they both slammed against the board.

Grant recovered quickly and managed to kick the ball to Cardosa, who then passed it to Silas.

The rookie should have run off down the field ready for the ball to come back at any moment, but he hesitated and looked at Emmeline with an adorably crinkled brow. "I didn't hurt you, did I?"

Her eyes narrowed. What was he doing talking to her? In the years she'd been coming to these games to watch her brother play, Emmeline had never known a player to stop and ask a fan if they were okay unless a stray ball hit a small child in the stands. Even then, they didn't always stop.

Since she was most definitely not a small child and the ball hadn't gone out of play, there was no reason for him to lose precious game minutes talking to her. And yet, she couldn't find her voice to tell him to get back on the field before Finn or Coach noticed. The minute his blue eyes met hers, she'd lost her voice.

"She's fine, Grant." Miriam pushed his shoulder over the boards. "Get moving."

Emmeline watched as he ran down the field toward the rest of the players, his mouth still turned down in confusion by her silence.

"What was *that*?" Miriam asked once he started playing again.

Emmeline blinked slowly. "What was what?"

"You know exactly what I'm talking about, so you can stop playing all innocent. You've got a crush on Grant." Miriam's lips curled into a sly grin.

"It's hard to have a crush on someone when you only found out they existed ten minutes ago."

Besides, Emmeline didn't get crushes at all. She was constantly working at her school, where most of her coworkers were women. Even when she wasn't, she didn't have a desire to date anyone—not anymore. While she didn't have an explanation for why she got all tongue-tied in front of Grant, she could absolutely, one-hundred percent say it was not because of a crush.

"No love at first sight?"

"Ew." She scrunched up her nose. "What is this? A cheesy rom-com? No, I don't love Grant Vaughn just because he almost bumped into me during a game. If that was the case, I would be madly in love with the entire team...minus Finn."

"That's too bad. I thought we could cheer on our boys together. It would be fun."

"We can still cheer on *the* boys together. My shouting just so happens to be from a strictly platonic standpoint."

The other team's coach called a time-out and both sides huddled together in their respective circles. Emmeline made a pointed effort not to look at Grant as he huddled with the other players just a few feet from where she stood.

Miriam turned her back to the field and leaned

against the board. "So, are you going to the after-party tonight?"

After-parties were community outreach events meant to connect players and fans. Since Emmeline already knew most of the team thanks to her brother, she didn't see the need to go. She shrugged. "I wasn't planning on it."

"Come on." Miriam sighed. "I haven't seen you all season. I miss you."

Emmeline bit her bottom lip. "I miss you too, but I don't know about tonight. I've got a lot of papers to grade." Even though it was true, it was a lame excuse.

"What about Finn?"

"What about him?"

"Don't you think he'd like to see his sister at City Bar?"

She laughed. "You act like I don't see Finn outside of sanctioned Storm events."

Miriam gave her sad puppy dog eyes. "But *I* don't get to see you outside of Storm events."

"Ugh." Emmeline was such a sucker. She threw her hands up. "Fine, I'll come to the after-party."

"Yay!"

"But only if you promise not to say another word about my crush on Grant."

The sly smile was back. "So, you're admitting that you do have a crush."

Emmeline gave her a hard look.

"Fine. No crush." She mimed zipping her lips, but Emmeline could see the corners of Miriam's mouth tugging up as she fought to keep from smiling. She was tempted to argue over it, but the ref blew his whistle and the game resumed.

The two girls turned their attention back to the arena. As the fast-paced match continued, Emmeline decided the after-party might not be such a bad idea. In fact, she was almost looking forward to it. Even though she wouldn't be some superfan looking to meet her heroes, it would be great to take a break from school for the night. She'd get to have more time with Miriam and Finn.

Maybe she'd see Grant there, maybe she wouldn't.

Though when he glanced at her halfway through the second quarter, she was definitely hoping she would.

GRANT

MAN, it felt good to get another Storm win under his belt.

Grant was still getting used to playing in the arena. The field was smaller, the game faster, and there were fewer players on the field. No matter how much he practiced in the arena, Grant still found himself adjusting to the new set of rules.

He must have been doing something right though, because Coach let him spend a lot of time playing instead of sitting and watching from the bench. Not too bad for a rookie.

Grant stripped off his sweaty top as he sat on the bench and tried to focus on the post-game speech from Coach. He was going over the highs and lows of the game while it was still fresh in everyone's minds, but all Grant could think about was getting back out there for the customary autograph session after the game. He wanted to see the fans—or more specifically, *one* fan.

He only hoped that the fact that she was sitting next to Miriam meant that he would get that chance. A seat in the VIP box meant that person loved the Storm, so she'd have to be there, right? Grant wasn't exactly sure what he planned to say, or do, if he saw the mystery girl at the autograph session, but he always worked best under pressure.

Coach continued to drone on and on. Grant thought he'd never stop. After yet another reminder of how the team needed to listen to Finn when he barked out orders during games, they were finally dismissed.

Grant immediately went to the sinks near the bathroom stalls. There wasn't enough time for a full fledged shower, but that didn't mean he needed to be completely disgusting when he went out there. He splashed water over his face and checked his reflection in the mirror. His hair was wet with sweat, so he stuck it under the faucet to rinse it out the best he could. He combed it back with his fingers. It would have to do.

Finn's reflection appeared behind him in the mirror. The team captain ran the palm of his hand over the top of Grant's head, undoing the progress he'd made. "Look at you. Who are you trying to impress?"

Grant felt his cheeks warm. It was tough enough being the new guy on the team—to the league. Having the captain catch him trying to look nice for a girl he'd never met wasn't something he wanted to admit. He pressed his lips together.

Finn's teasing smile fell. "I'm sorry, man. You got a girlfriend out there?"

He shook his head. "No girlfriend." He'd only been in Florida for a couple months, and that time had been jam-packed with learning the area, the game, and attending practices. Even if he wanted to date, there just wasn't the time.

"Wait." Finn's eyes went wide. "Are you trying to look nice for a *fan*?"

Finn's voice echoed off the walls of the locker room causing several heads to turn in their direction.

Just great.

Grant ignored the question and smoothed down the pieces of hair that were now sticking up in a million different directions. When he was satisfied, he pushed past Finn to avoid the stares from his teammates.

"Hey, Grant," Finn called.

Grant stopped and turned.

Finn jogged over and lowered his voice. "Listen, I get it. Having hot girls come out and cheer you on is a nice perk of playing professionally. But be careful. Some of those girls are crazy. If you don't believe me, ask Silas."

Grant nodded before he turned and walked out of the locker room toward the field. It's not like he was looking for something serious. He was busy trying to keep up with the hustle of being a rookie. He had to prove himself to the team, work on his branding, and at some point do something with his degree. That piece of paper saying he graduated magna cum laude wasn't going to do him any good if it collected dust for the foreseeable future. With so much on his plate, he barely had time to shower, let alone time for a relationship.

And yet, he still wanted to talk to *her*. There wasn't any harm in that. A friendly conversation—maybe grabbing a bite at the food truck rally together—wouldn't derail his vision.

When he made it back out to the arena, the Storm staff had just finished putting long tables at midfield for the autograph session. Now, they were bringing out chairs. Grant grabbed a metal folding chair and walked out onto the field. He sat down toward the middle of the tables, so that he'd be able to see most of the fans as they spilled onto the field in a few minutes. It was his fifth time signing, and it was still his favorite part. Playing was great but interacting with the fans was better than scoring the winning goal.

Finn set a chair next to Grant and flopped down in it. "Look, I'm sorry for calling you out in front of everyone."

Grant shook his head and reached out to grab the black Sharpie in front of him. "Don't worry about it."

"It's been a few years since I was a rookie, but I remember what a crazy time it was. Getting involved with a fan is bad news." Finn's head turned back and forth as he looked around before turning back to Grant. "Trust me."

"You dated a fan?"

Finn gave him a tight smile in return. "It's almost never a good idea. Just be careful."

Was that a yes or a no? Grant hoped that he would elaborate, but Finn spent the next few minutes hollering out at the rest of the guys. They trickled onto the field and found open seats at the autograph table.

Grant looked up at the countdown timer on the wall. Less than two minutes until the fans hanging out on the perimeter of the arena would rush the field with their shirts and trinkets. Not wanting to get another lecture, he tried to act natural. His eyes scanned the office staff as they milled around the field.

Miriam was standing close to Silas. They were laughing about something, when Silas reached out and tucked a strand of Miriam's blonde hair behind her ear. It was no surprise to see Miriam out here—it was her job, after all—but Grant wanted to see her friend. The girl with the red ponytail and gorgeous eyes.

His gaze went back to the fans, slowly moving over the people waiting just outside the arena where the goal's net was rolled up. A flash of red hair caught his attention. It was her. She was here. He sat up in his seat and pushed back his hair.

When the buzzer rang out through the arena, he lost the mystery girl in the flurry of action that followed.

A bunch of kids holding soccer balls ran in front of him. "Will you sign these?"

Grant smiled at them. "Of course." He ran the point of the marker across the smooth surface of the soccer ball to sign his name with the number seven underneath it.

The boys all took turns pushing to the front, practically shoving their balls at Grant when it was their turn. Once they were all signed, they shouted their thanks before moving on to the next player down the line.

Jerseys and cups all became a blur. Grant tried to give everyone the attention they deserved until things slowed down. Lines got much shorter, even non-existent for some players.

Once they got their autographs, most fans left—either to go home or to the after-party at City Bar. The players themselves would only stay out on the field for a couple more minutes then they would do the same.

Grant had given up hope that he would see his mystery girl, when he spotted her in Finn's line. There were a couple people in front of her, which meant she'd be right next to Finn—and Grant—in just a couple minutes.

There was no one in his line and Grant tried to keep his eyes from wandering to where she stood. He looked down at the marker in his hands and twisted the cap. It wasn't his usual style to be attracted to someone so quickly. What was it about this girl?

When she made her way to the front of the line, Finn stood up. He leaned over the table to give her a hug—a long, familiar hug.

"Good game," she said as they pulled apart.

Finn didn't immediately sit back down. Instead, he jerked his chin at the jersey she wore. "Nice shirt."

She looked down with mock surprise. "Oh, this old thing?"

"This old thing" happened to be a one-of-a-kind game day jersey from last week's themed night game. They were auctioned off with the proceeds going to a local charity. The guys had all watched the online bidding, joking about who was the most popular by how high the bids had gone. Even though Grant was new to the team, somehow he hadn't gotten last place.

Not that it really mattered. Finn's final price had beaten them all in a landslide thanks to a bidding war in the last thirty minutes. There were only a few reasons people paid that much for a jersey.

There was a sly smile on her face. "It cost a fortune, so I figured I might as well get it signed."

Finn laughed and motioned for her to turn around. When she did, he signed the back with his marker. "You act like you weren't going to see me unless you came tonight."

She laughed and spun back around. "But you know I love seeing you play."

"Funny, because I haven't seen you at a game all season."

Neither had Grant. He would have remembered her for sure.

She started into a long explanation about work being busy, and how she promised to do better for the rest of the home games. She started recapping some of her favorite plays from the game when a family appeared in front of Grant. They pulled out their ticket stubs and asked if he would sign them.

Grant barely resisted the urge to shush the little girl who was telling him how he was her favorite player, hating that he was missing the conversation between Finn and the redhead. But when he looked down at the girl's gap-tooth grin, Grant felt a pang of guilt. He should be thrilled to know that he was someone's favorite player his first season playing in the MASL. He racked his brain trying to find a way to make this encounter special for the little girl standing in front of him.

He could offer to sign her shirt, but since it wasn't specifically Storm, that wasn't exactly fitting. He could take a picture with her, but again, that wasn't above and beyond. That was something he'd already done with three other fans that night.

An idea suddenly came to him. When the girl finished listing all the reasons she loved Grant, he gave her a big grin. "It's great to know I have such a loyal fan. Are you coming to next week's game?"

The little girl turned around and looked at her mom. "Are we?"

Her mom gave her a sad smile and looked over at the girl's father.

He shook his head. "Sorry, sweetie. We can't go to every game. Coming tonight was a special treat."

Grant wished he could decipher what "special treat" meant. Was it a money thing? If so, his idea was perfect. He got a certain number of free tickets to give to friends for each game, and since he didn't really know anyone other than his teammates, they always went to waste.

He stood up and jerked his chin at the girl's father, hoping he would lean in over the table so he could ask him quietly. Grant had gotten enough lectures from his older sister about giving his nieces treats without first asking their parents first.

The dad's brows furrowed, but he leaned in.

Grant kept his voice low. "I've got free tickets for next week's game if you'd like them."

The other man leaned back and shook his head. "No, I couldn't."

Grant lifted his brows. "Because you can't come?"

"Because I don't want to take advantage."

"It's hard to take advantage when I'm offering." Grant chuckled and pulled out his phone. "Why don't you give me your last name. I'll make sure they're waiting for you guys at the box office next week before the game."

"That's really generous of you."

Grant shrugged. "It's the least I can do for such an enthusiastic fan."

The little girl tugged on her dad's arm. "What are you guys talking about?"

Her dad smiled down at her. "Grant Vaughn just gave us tickets for next week's game."

The girl jumped up and down. "Really?"

Grant leaned across the table so his face was on her level. "Yep. But you have to cheer really loud when you come. Deal?"

Her smile widened. "Deal."

The dad gave him their last name and thanked Grant one more time before the family walked off. Free tickets weren't much, but Grant was happy that it meant so much to them. The idea of doing something special for them gave him a warm feeling in his chest.

He'd even successfully forgotten about the mystery girl for a couple minutes. That was, until he looked over at Finn. The line in front of him was empty, and the girl was gone.

Finn smiled at him. "That was pretty cool of you, man. Giving them those tickets. I'm sure that family appreciates it."

Grant rubbed the back of his neck as a small smile touched his lips. "Yeah, well, after hearing that I was that girl's favorite player, I didn't really have a choice, did I?"

"You always have a choice." He slapped Grant's back. "But focus on those kinds of fans and making them happy, and you'll be fine."

Grant's smile fell. He could read between the lines. Finn was once again telling him not to get involved with fans. Not that the captain was very good at following his own advice.

There was obviously something going on between Finn and the gorgeous redhead. The connection they had with one another was obvious, even in that small exchange. Grant was surprised by the sadness that came with the realization.

He didn't know that girl, but he had wanted to.

Too bad that his captain was dating her, and she was completely off-limits.

3

GRANT

GRANT WAS LESS eager to get to City Bar after finding out that the girl he wanted to talk to was dating Finn, but he'd already agreed to go. Plus, a drink to celebrate the Storm's win might not be so bad right now. He and Vinny swung by the team house to get proper showers before driving to the bar.

Grant was thankful for the house that the owners of the team provided for players who lived out of town. Living there meant he didn't have to pay double rent for the months he spent in Florida—for his apartment back home and here—though he didn't always love the lack of privacy that came with living with three other guys in the four-bedroom place. Sure, he got his own bedroom, but it felt like the other guys were always there.

Sometimes it was so unbearable he had to go out to a local park or coffee shop just to breathe.

Getting dressed only took minutes—a Storm tee, jeans, and Chucks seemed like the perfect thing to wear to a bar—and they drove over in record time. His hair was still wet when he and Vinny walked inside. Some fans cheered when they saw them.

Grant smiled and waved. Fans lifted their drinks to toast them, but quickly returned to their conversations with the people sitting at their tables.

"Shall we?" Grant jerked his head at the bar.

Vinny nodded. "You know it."

The hot-headed defender ordered two shots, both for himself, while Grant just got a beer. Most of the players took it easy when it came to drinking—especially during the season. They relied on their bodies being in peak shape so that they were able to play their best.

Vinny...well, he happened to be the anomaly. He would drink heavily all night, wake up bright and early without even the slightest headache, and be ready to give it his all for the group workout—assuming someone didn't piss him off about whatever random thing made him feel explosive that day.

The defender kicked back both shots, slammed the small glasses on the table, and walked over to a table filled with fans.

Grant grabbed his pint and faced the rest of the bar. Though not everyone was there for the after party, a large number of the people mingling were wearing green and black—the Storm's colors. He wished he had the confidence to walk over to a table full of strangers and talk like Vinny, but Grant still felt so new. He worried about what to say. He didn't know the team history and stats like the die-hard fans here did.

Hell, he'd been completely oblivious to the Silas drama at the beginning of the season. Grant didn't realize that Silas used to play for the Storm until he'd overheard it in the locker room after one of their first practices. Now at the bar with fans, he was worried he would say—or do—the wrong thing and look like an idiot.

Grant's gaze moved around the room until they landed on a small booth off in a corner. On one side were Miriam and Silas. On the other were Finn and the gorgeous redhead. They were talking excitedly and laughing like they were all the best of friends.

"It's weird to see Finn and Silas acting like they didn't have a grudge for the first part of the season, isn't it?"

Grant turned his head to find Bastian standing beside him. The veteran player lifted his glass of water at Grant.

Grant lifted his beer before turning back to the double date in the booth. Finn was laughing at something his date was saying. "I don't think I've ever seen Finn look so happy."

Bastian shrugged. "Yeah, Emmeline has a way of bringing out that part of him."

Emmeline.

It was nice to finally have a name to go along with the face, not that it would do Grant any good now. Just seeing the two interact made it obvious that they loved each other. When Emmeline leaned her head on Finn's shoulder, Grant turned his entire body so that it faced Bastian. "How long have they been dating?"

Bastian, who had taken a sip of his water, started to

choke. The choke soon became a hearty laugh. "Dating? They're not dating."

"But..." Grant lowered his brows as he glanced in their direction once more. They looked awfully comfortable together.

"Emmeline is Finn's sister."

Grant's cheeks flushed. Oh course she was. Now that he looked at them, he could see the resemblance. While Finn's hair was more auburn and Emmeline's a brighter red, they both had similar complexions, and their noses were the same.

"But Finn is going to die when he hears that you thought they were dating. Florida can be pretty messed up, but we draw the line at first cousins."

Grant laughed to cover his embarrassment at his mistake. "And how much is it going to take for you to keep your mouth shut?"

"Oh, no." Bastian shook his head and smiled with pure glee. "This is way too good not to share."

He groaned. "Seriously?"

"Come on, it's funny."

"And embarrassing. I hate that I keep making all these rookie mistakes."

"Alright. It'll be our little secret." He slapped Grant's back. "I'm going to go talk to some fans for a bit. Enjoy your beer, but make sure you do the same. Fans come out to these events because they want to interact with us, not watch us talk to each other."

Grant looked down at his drink and nodded. "Yeah, okay."

With an encouraging smile, Bastian walked off and started talking to some people on the other end of the bar. Once Grant was alone, he allowed the wave of embarrassment to wash over him. The number of mistakes he'd made was piling up by the minute.

At least it wasn't all bad. He'd not only found out Emmeline's name but also that she wasn't off-limits because she was dating Finn. This was good.

But not nearly as good as when Emmeline walked up to the bar a couple feet from where he stood. She leaned up against the wood countertop and waited for the bartender to notice her. It didn't take long—shocker—and once she finished ordering a margarita, Grant closed the distance between them. "Hey."

She looked up and gave him a small smile. "Hey."

"I'm Grant."

She turned her gaze back toward the bar. "I know."

"Oh yeah?" Feeling bold by her admission, he leaned against the counter next to her.

A small smile tugged at her lips. "It helps when your name is on the back of your jersey."

"But I'm not wearing my jersey."

"You had it on at the game."

"It says Vaughn, not Grant."

She turned her head and looked at him again, the smile on her lips growing slightly. "Fine. After you stopped playing in the middle of the game, I asked Miriam who you were."

He waggled his brows. "So you were asking about me?"

Still smiling, Emmeline rolled her eyes. "Don't flatter yourself."

Grant pressed his hand against his chest. "Ouch."

She rolled her eyes.

But the smile on her lips encouraged him to press his luck further. "Wanna hear a secret?"

Emmeline lifted a brow.

He leaned in a little and lowered his voice. "I was asking about you too."

Her eyes narrowed. "Should I be worried?"

"Nah, I was just wondering who that pretty girl sitting next to Finn was. Emmeline, right?" He flashed a smile.

Instead of smiling back, she kept a flat expression and stuck out her hand. Grant shook it, feeling oddly formal. "My friends call me Em."

Did that include him? "Nice to officially meet you, *Em*." He waited to see if she would tell him to call her by her full name.

She didn't.

Before either of them could say anything else, the bartender returned with Em's drink. He set the glass on a coaster in front of her. "Do you want to run a tab?"

"I'm only getting the one drink." She slid her purse from her shoulder and started digging around inside. "I'll just pay now."

Grant put his hand on her arm. "Let me get it."

Em's hand stilled as she looked down at where they touched. "You don't have to do that."

"I want to."

"But—"

"Put it on my tab," he said to the bartender, not giving Em the chance to argue.

"Sure thing." The man nodded at him before walking off to talk to another customer.

Em put her purse back on her shoulder, pulling away from his hand. Her eyes were trained on the drink in front of her. "That was really nice, but you should know I don't date players."

Grant pushed down his disappointment and leaned in. "It's just a drink. You could say thank you and leave it at that."

Her lips twitched. "Thank you."

He stretched his arms and turned to face the room, elbows on the bar. "Besides, I'm not looking to date either."

Though I would have made an exception for you.

She faced Grant with wide eyes. "You aren't?"

"Nah, I was just happy to make amends for bumping into you earlier."

Em stared at him another moment before a corner of her mouth lifted. "If I got free drinks every time someone bumped into me, I might start leaning over the boards during games."

"If you started leaning over the boards during games, I might not be able to pay attention to the ball."

She pressed her lips together. "You know you're not doing a very good job of stating your case of not hitting on me with comments like that, right?"

"And you know that a little flirting doesn't mean I'm trying to date you, right?"

That was a lie. Grant was thoroughly enjoying their playful exchange and wanted more.

Em laughed softly. Looking at him through lowered lashes, she jerked her head toward the booth. "I should probably get back to everyone before Finn sends out the search party. Bye, Grant."

This place wasn't so big, and Finn could see her from his spot in the booth, but Grant nodded. "I'll see you around, Em."

With his back pressed against the counter, Grant rested his elbows on the bar and watched as Em returned to her seat. She was only a few feet away when Bastian stepped directly in front of him blocking his view. "What do you think you're doing?"

Grant grinned. "Doing what you said. Interacting with the fans."

Bastian scowled. "Didn't you hear me when I said that she's his sister?"

"I did." And Grant was thrilled with that bit of information.

He'd thought Em was off-limits because she was dating Finn. Knowing that the mutual adoration he'd seen on hers and Finn's faces was strictly sibling love was great. And to think he might have missed out on talking to her if Bastian hadn't cleared that up.

Grant craned his head around Bastian to try to get another glance at Em.

"That makes her off-limits."

Grant's head snapped back toward Bastian. "What are you talking about?"

"Finn's really protective over his little sister." Bastian rubbed the bridge of his nose. "You're new, so let me make this one thing crystal clear before you do something dumb. You cannot date Emmeline O'Brien."

This had to be some kind of joke. Grant laughed. "Not sure what century you're living in, but my sister would tear me a new one if I tried to tell her who she could and couldn't date."

"I'm serious. This dude, Parrera, tried to date Emmeline without permission and ended up with a broken nose."

Grant's smile fell. "Sounds a little extreme." He glanced over at the booth just in time to see a guy stop by the table. Finn gave the man a fierce look that said go away. Grant swallowed hard.

Having also witnessed the exchange, Bastian shook his head. "Like I said, he's very protective of her."

Grant opened his mouth to ask more about it, but Silas started hollering in their direction.

"Bastian, get over here! You still owe me a rematch in darts."

"I'll be right there!" Bastian turned and faced Grant once more, his face hard. "Consider this your one and only warning."

Without another word, Bastian walked over to where everyone sat together. A minute later, Silas and Bastian were taking turns throwing darts at a board on the wall while Miriam cheered them on.

Grant took a long sip of his beer as he glanced over to where Finn and Em remained in the booth. He wondered what Finn's deal was. Breaking someone's nose because they tried to date your sister sounded more like something Vinny would do—not their cool-headed captain.

But it would make sense if that was the reason Em didn't date players. Not wanting a repeat of that, she might have thought it was easier to avoid athletes altogether.

Grant would just need to feel out Finn and see if he still felt that way. It was possible that Finn had relaxed since that incident happened. If that was the case, maybe he could convince Em that it was okay to date players.

But he wasn't looking to date her, was he?

The more he replayed their flirtatious encounter, and the more he observed her through the night, her red hair drawing his eye and her eyes sparkling with laughter as she teased her brother, the more he realized that he did want...something.

Maybe dating, maybe not, but definitely more than one bar conversation with Emmeline. Now, he just needed to find out how to make that happen.

4

EMMELINE

THERE WAS a reason people hated Mondays.

Half the class forgot their homework, three kids fell asleep at their desks, one had thrown up all over Em's shoes, and that was all before lunch. Teaching wasn't always the easiest job, but Em enjoyed being in the classroom and making a difference in these children's lives.

But Mondays were still Mondays, no matter how much you loved your job.

With so many of her third graders dealing with struggles too difficult for their age, Em was happy she could be a bright spot in their lives. She just didn't like being the spot in the middle of the bullseye when it came to projectile vomit. Her students were lucky she didn't start dry heaving right then and there.

Thankfully, the bell had rung only moments after. She sent her students to the lunchroom with a fellow teacher and had raced to the bathroom.

After wiping her shoes down with enough sanitizing wipes to clean her entire room, she finally walked into the teacher's lounge. Frida, who taught art, was already in their usual spot. There was a small splatter of red paint on the front of her plain cotton jumper. Her dark hair was piled on top of her head in a messy bun, but her makeup was immaculate enough to put any beauty blogger to shame. The plastic salad bowl in front of her was almost empty.

"I was wondering where you were. It's not like these twenty-five-minute lunch breaks give a lot of time to gallivant all over campus," Frida said when she noticed Em walking toward her.

Em plopped down across the table from her and set a peanut butter and jelly sandwich on the table. "It's been a day."

A corner of Frida's mouth lifted. "It's only eleven."

"Yeah, and I could already use a nap." Em quickly filled Frida in on the drama from that morning.

When she was done, Frida wrinkled her nose. "And you're still eating after all that?"

"I think I'm going to fall over if I don't. I feel like I'm running on fumes today."

Frida put her elbow on the table and propped her chin in her hand. "Exciting weekend working on lesson plans?"

Em rolled her eyes.

"Wait, don't tell me." Frida sat up in her seat. "You spent hours online looking for cute ways to teach the kids about dividing while I got to work on my latest sculpture and have it count as research."

"For your information, I went out on Saturday night, and stayed out way too late." Between Silas and Finn's jokes and following Grant around the bar with her eyes, she'd lost track of time and didn't realize it was two in the morning until they did last call.

"As your best friend since kindergarten, I know you didn't have a date this weekend. And last time I checked, Storm games didn't run that late." Frida sent a teasing smile at Em before stabbing her fork into another bite of lettuce.

"I ended up hanging out with Finn at City Bar."

Frida stopped chewing. "You were with Finn?"

"Yeah. I haven't seen him in, like, forever."

"Talk about anything important?"

"Not really. But spending the entire night with him made it easier not to talk to another player."

Frida started eating again. "So, who weren't you trying to talk to?"

She averted her gaze as she took a bite of her sandwich and said, "No one."

"Wait." Frida set her fork down and stared at her. "This wasn't just not talking to someone because you didn't feel like being social. What happened?"

Em pressed her lips together. If she wasn't so tired, she wouldn't have been so obvious about it. Of course, she'd planned to tell Frida eventually, she'd just hoped to get through this day first. "Promise not to laugh?"

"I make no such promise, but you'd better tell me anyway."

She let out a long sigh before she told Frida about how Grant had bumped into her at the game. When she got to the part where they flirted at the bar, Frida's eyes went wide.

"Is he cute?"

Instead of answering out loud she pulled out her phone, opened Instagram, and typed in Grant's name. Once his profile was up, she squeezed her eyes shut, took a deep breath, and slid the phone across the table toward Frida.

A few seconds went by, and Em realized she was still holding her breath while she waited for her best friend's response. She released it and looked up at Frida.

Frida's eyes were glued to the screen, and her lips slowly curved up into a smile. "Ooh. I can see why you like him."

Em reached out and snatched the phone from Frida's hand. She cradled it to her chest and glared at Frida. "I don't *like* him."

"It's okay if you do. He's gorgeous." She wiggled her perfectly groomed brows.

"He is." Her cheeks warmed at the admission.

"And you were avoiding him because of your no-dating-athletes rule."

"Obviously."

Frida was silent for a moment. "You know that not every guy is Travis, right?"

Travis.

Hearing his name brought back so many painful memories—memories Em had worked hard to forget. Not only had Travis destroyed her heart, he'd made it impossible for her to trust another guy for years. She pressed the heel of her hand against her forehead trying to clear her mind.

Frida put a hand on her arm. "Sorry, I shouldn't have mentioned him."

"It's okay." It had been six years since Travis had shown his true colors. It was time to move past it. She looked up at Frida. "But it's not just him. Remember Mark in college? Or Damien?" Every athlete she'd taken a chance on was a complete waste of space.

Frida snorted. "Damien was ridiculous."

"Yeah, he was. But Damien was also a reminder to stay strong in my convictions and not get distracted by a pretty pair of pecs, because there is literally nothing hiding behind them but a self-love that rivals Narcissus."

"Dang, girl, tell me how you really feel."

"Don't you remember how bad that date was?"

"I remember."

Damien had chosen a restaurant that Em hated and talked about himself the entire time. When the bill came, he insisted that they split the cost fifty-fifty even though his meal cost twice as much. And when they'd discovered Em's car battery had died, he told her he couldn't wait around. Apparently, there had been a game on that night, and he hadn't wanted to miss any of it.

Em had been forced to call her brother to come rescue her. He'd come right away and even took her out for ice cream on the way home. Finn was the perfect big brother who was always there for her.

Her date with Damien had been the last straw. After that, Em had decided no more athletes—soccer players especially. It was a good rule that had protected her heart.

She gave Frida a pointed look. "So you know why the rule is in place."

"I do." She shrugged. "Finn's not like that."

Em shook her head. "He's my brother. What's your point?"

"My point is that not every athlete is a jerk. Finn's one of the good ones. Maybe Grant is too."

"I don't think it's worth the risk."

"Well, you know what is worth the risk?" Frida asked, her voice cheery once more. She pulled out her phone and started tapping the screen.

Em's heart dropped in her stomach. "What are you doing?"

"Someone took their phone back before I could look at all of Grant's pictures," she said without looking up from her screen. "I'm gonna finish snooping."

"Stop it." Em leaned over the table and tried to grab Frida's phone.

Frida leaned back in her chair just out of reach. She laughed. "What are you? Twelve?"

"No." She sat back down in her seat and pouted. Great, now Em was acting like she was twelve. "Just don't follow him, okay?"

"Too late." Frida gave Em an innocent look that was anything but.

Em covered her face with her hands. There were so many pictures of the two friends posing together on Frida's page. If Grant looked at Frida's profile, he would see Em. Then he'd know for sure that she'd been stalking his profile after meeting him this past weekend.

She was going to kill Frida, but the lunch bell rang before she got the chance.

Em gathered her things from the table and looked at Frida. "Please promise me you won't play matchmaker and message him."

Frida set her phone down. "Do you really think you need to say that?"

Em stood up and sighed. Frida always teased about Em needing to get a boyfriend, but Em was ninety-nine percent sure that she would never do anything to embarrass her. "No."

"Good." Frida's wicked smile was the reason for the one percent uncertainty. "Then I'll see you later."

Em waved at her friend as she threw away her trash and walked to grab her students from the lunchroom, determined not to worry about Frida or Grant anymore today—only that her clothes remained puke-free.

THE REST of the day was fine until class was done for the day. When the dismissal bell rang, one boy remained in her class. His arms folded on his desk, and his head rested face down on top of them so that Em could only see his blond hair. He was supposed to go to aftercare until his mom finished working in the cafeteria, though this wasn't the first time he'd stayed behind in her class.

Em took a deep breath before she sat down on the desk beside him. "Riley?"

The young boy sniffed a few times but didn't say anything.

Em's heart broke for him. His dad had died last year, and while she hadn't known him the year before, everyone said he wasn't the same boy. Based on what other teachers had said, he'd gone from a happy and silly kid to a quiet one who kept to himself.

The quiet kid was the only Riley that Em had known.

She hated that he'd experienced such a devastating loss at a young age. If it was possible to take his pain and make it her own, Em would do it in a heartbeat. But she couldn't. All she could do was be a consistent presence in his life and offer comfort when he needed it.

She reached out, put her hand on his back and rubbed it in circles hoping to soothe him. Slowly, his muscles relaxed, and the sniffles became few and far between.

Riley pushed up and rubbed the back of his hands over his eyes. His gaze stayed trained to the floor. "Sorry, Ms. O'Brien."

"Sweetie, you don't have to be sorry." She leaned in. "Wanna talk about it?"

He shook his head. "Not really."

"That's fine. You don't have to talk to me, but if you ever want to, I'm always happy to listen, okay?"

Without looking up, he nodded.

She knew that she should send him to aftercare, but he looked like he was barely keeping it together. The idea of him crying and kids making fun of him was too much to bear. "Do you want to stay and help me tidy until your mom finishes up? I can text her and let her know you're here."

He nodded again.

"Great," she said, trying to keep the pity out of her voice. "You can wipe down desks or sharpen pencils. Whatever you want."

Riley got up from his seat and grabbed the canister of sanitizing wipes from her desk and went to the far end of the room. Once he did, Em pulled out her phone and sent a quick text to his mom to let her know where her son was.

Notifications from Instagram flashed on her screen. It had been fun to look at Grant's pictures earlier, but now she just felt guilty for doing that. It felt wrong to enjoy herself when there was so much pain in the world. She just wanted to go around and fix it.

Frida had warned her time and time again that she would burn out if she wasn't careful. She'd told Em that she needed to put a wall between herself and her kids. Not a stone wall that didn't allow for meaningful connections, but Em needed to be able to separate herself from the constant onslaught of emotions that came with teaching so that she could recharge and be the very best teacher for these kids.

Em knew that Frida was right. She couldn't fix everything and everyone.

But that didn't mean she couldn't make every effort to be the best teacher she could be. That started with getting rid of unnecessary distractions. She swiped the notifications left to delete them and started cleaning with Riley.

GRANT

GRANT PULLED his shirt off over his head and wiped his face.

He never thought body weight exercises could be so tough, but Finn had a way of pushing everyone when it came to agility training. They'd been going at it for an hour at Big Results, the gym where the players all went. Grant's muscles were beginning to feel like Jell-O, and he was sure he'd lost half his body weight in sweat.

But he still wasn't done. He still needed to post something online to build up his online presence.

He really wished he would have taken some videos of his workouts before he was as sweaty—and tired—as he was, but he'd shown up to practice late and didn't want to ask anyone to stop what they were doing to record him.

Grant grabbed a fresh shirt from his gym bag and put it on before he scanned the room for someone who might help. Some of the other players had already left, while others were still running through drills. Finally, his eyes landed on his mark.

"Hey, Cardosa," he called out. The offensive player was sitting in the corner mixing a post-workout shake that was meant to build muscles. "Will you come help me with something real quick?"

"Sure thing." Cardosa hopped up from his spot and walked over, his drink in hand. "You want me to record you doing a workout?"

Grant rubbed a hand over the back of his neck. Was he that predictable?

"Don't be embarrassed. Silas has nagged every single player about 'building an online presence.' I'm pretty sure we've all tried it at some point. Just tell me what you need."

"Thanks." Grant smiled as he scouted out a place to set up. "Let's go over there."

Cardosa followed him to a side of the room without any other players. When he was ready, he signaled to Cardosa to start recording. Giving it everything he had, Grant ran through some drills. Jumping jacks, squats, push-ups, lunges, sit-ups, and finally burpees. By the end, he was nauseated, but he'd done it and somehow managed to maintain proper form in the process.

He grabbed a towel and wiped his face once more before he looked over to Cardosa.

His teammate grimaced. "I'm so sorry. I forgot to hit record."

Now Grant really did think he was going to throw up. It was only one workout, but he'd pushed himself hard. He hoped it would gain more followers, and that somehow Em would see it and be impressed.

Cardosa started laughing. "Oh, man. Your reaction was priceless."

Grant threw his sweaty towel at him. "That's not funny."

"It's pretty funny," Silas said walking over. "It doesn't matter how many times Cardosa pulls that stunt, I laugh every time."

Grant stalked over to Cardosa and grabbed his phone out of his hand. "And here I was feeling special."

"Like I said, Silas pushes everyone to post their workouts. Since I refuse to do it, I get my kicks at everyone else's expense."

"You handled it much better than some of the other guys." Silas slapped Grant's back.

"They all know better now, so I haven't done it in a while." Cardosa's eyes quickly went to the defender and back to Grant. "And I refuse to mess with Vinny."

Silas wrapped an arm around Cardosa. "That's because you're a lover, not a fighter, aren't you?"

Cardosa stepped out of Silas' reach. "If you keep insisting on hugging me, I might make an exception." Silas laughed it off.

Watching their playful fight was much better than seeing what would happen if Cardosa had decided to prank Vinny instead. "The Box" surely would have thrown a sucker punch that would put the whole team in a mood. He had a bad attitude, and Grant was convinced that if Vinny wasn't such a good player, no one would put up with his crap.

"Seriously, though. You're doing a great job of building your brand."

Cardosa snickered beside him.

Silas shot him a look. "Don't listen to him. He's just upset he's not as good as me."

"Your overinflated opinion of yourself never ceases to amaze." Cardosa chuckled and grabbed his stuff. "Grant, you need anything else?"

When he shook his head, Cardosa walked off.

"You're putting the work in at every practice, and everyone can see that," Silas said. "We're lucky to have you on the team."

Grant filled with pride at the compliment. He and Silas hadn't started the season on the best terms—Grant had thought Silas was trying to sabotage the rest of the players when in reality he was just trying to get his ex to fall back in love with him.

Now that things were cleared up, he saw Silas as a bit of a mentor. The veteran player had been in the league for five years and was one of the top scorers on the team. Though they played different positions, Grant looked to him for advice.

"Thanks, man."

Silas pointed to the phone in Grant's hand. "Don't forget to post that. You want to post often and try to get engagement. That's how you get companies to notice you. Once they do, they'll start sending you free stuff. If they like what you do with it, they'll start paying you."

"Like Protein Life?"

"Exactly." Silas nodded. "Thanks to them signing me on as a featured athlete, I have multiple income streams. If anything were to happen and I couldn't play anymore, they'd help keep food on the table while I found something else."

Having another source of income sounded amazing. As a rookie, his pay barely covered the bills. He could start delivering pizza part-time or pick up some day labor shifts working in construction—a lot of the players admitted to doing that their first year. Using his business degree would definitely help him financially, but Grant wanted to focus on the sport and almost any job in that field would take way more time than a delivery route.

If he followed Silas' advice and built a brand around soccer and his workouts, he'd be able to have some extra cash for doing what he loved.

He sat down on a bench and watched the video Cardosa had taken of him running through his workout. He looked good despite wanting to throw up the entire time from pushing so hard.

Grant knew he'd get a lot of likes, so he pulled up Instagram on his phone. Silas insisted it was the best platform for attracting fitness companies. He posted the video and, because he couldn't help himself, he pulled up Frida Hall's account.

At first, Grant hadn't given her a second thought. He gained followers everyday thanks to Silas' advice. But when she liked several of his posts all at once, he'd visited her profile. After a quick glance at her pictures, he was glad he had. Frida Hall was friends with Emmeline O'Brien. He knew that because she was in about half of Frida's posts, smiling brightly in each of them.

She was just as gorgeous as he remembered.

Was she talking about him to Frida? He had to imagine she was since Frida had started following him only days after he and Em had met at City Bar. Until now, Grant had been too afraid to request to follow her private account, not wanting to look like a crazy stalker.

But after posting his workout—which had already gained a lot of views and likes—he felt bold. He hit request and waited. It wasn't like following her on Instagram was trying to date her.

When he went back to Frida's profile and looked at Emmeline's smile, however, he wondered if he'd ever be satisfied with just being her friend.

6

EMMELINE

"HOW'S GRANT'S Instagram looking today?" Frida asked Emmeline softly.

The two of them were sitting in the back of the auditorium as the school's principal held an assembly about fundraising. The entire school would sell candy bars to earn money for special programs—like art supplies for Frida's class.

Em turned her screen off and put her phone in her pocket. She kept her eyes trained on the stage. "I-I wasn't looking at Instagram. I was responding to a parent's email."

That was a boldfaced lie. Em had been looking at a picture of Grant that showed off the tattoos on his left arm. Thankfully, the darkness of the room hid the way she'd been drooling over it. What was it about boys and ink?

She'd tried not to look at it very often, but once he'd requested to follow her account, it was like the dam burst.

She'd followed him back and scrolled down through all his old posts. They were mostly about workouts—which wasn't necessarily bad.

But when she went back even further, she found pre-Storm Grant.

She liked pre-Storm Grant for a host of reasons that didn't involve his muscles or his tattoos.

For one, family was important to him. There were quite a few pictures of him with his parents, his sister, and his nieces in his hometown of Kansas City. He never looked embarrassed to have his arm over his mom's shoulder when they posed for the camera, and the smile on his face when he was with his nieces was sweet and genuine.

Then there was his time in college. She loved seeing his personality in his posts about studying for finals, wandering around downtown Macon, and hanging out with his college friends.

Not only that, his older posts were cheesy. He had a tendency to use puns and dad jokes as his captions, and Em enjoyed seeing that part of him. The part of Grant that wasn't so...athletic.

Like when he'd dressed up like Dwight from the office the previous Halloween. His caption read: **Is it bad that I actually like *Battlestar Galactica*?**

It was one of her all-time favorite shows, and she'd never known another person to feel the same way about it. Sure, Frida had given it a gallant effort but stopped after six episodes. She'd binge-watched the remaining seventy by herself—sometimes forgetting to sleep.

She couldn't believe Mr. Soccer really enjoyed it, so she'd tested him and commented: **Prove it**.

Five minutes later, he'd sent her a DM with the names of the Final Five Cylons—in the order they were revealed.

After that, Em knew she was in trouble. She didn't send anymore DMs, too afraid to get to know him better, but she enjoyed looking every day to see if he posted something new. And every time she posted, she felt a thrill waiting for him to like it.

"What did they want?" Frida asked.

Em looked over. "Huh?"

"The parents you were just emailing. What did they want?"

Her face burned. "Oh, to schedule a conference."

"A conference. Is that what they're calling it these days?" Frida leaned in close and whispered, "I'm sure you wouldn't mind a little one-on-one time with Grant."

"I wasn't..." Em leaned back in the hard, plastic chair. "Fine, I was looking at his Instagram. Happy?"

Frida shook her head causing her dark curls to bounce. "I'd be a lot happier if you didn't feel the need to hide it from me. You act like I don't see the way you're both treating the app like it's Match.com."

Em sat up and looked around to see if any of the other teachers had heard Frida. Her best friend teasing her was one thing, but Em didn't want her coworkers to overhear them talk about a dating site—especially since she wasn't on one. She narrowed her eyes at Frida.

"I follow you both. I see the way you like each other's posts." Frida paused. "And the way you've gone from posting once a week to every day."

"I can't help that I've recently discovered my love of selfies."

Frida snorted. "You don't have to explain it to me, you know. You're allowed to have a crush."

Em really wished everyone would stop using that word. What was going on between her and Grant wasn't a crush. It was more like low-key flirting. Something just between them. They didn't have to acknowledge anything was happening—because nothing was—but it was nice to know that there was a guy out there who thought about her every once in a while.

"So, I was thinking about coming to the game tonight," Frida said, changing the subject.

"You are?" Her eyes went back up to the stage as their principal started listing the prizes for the top sellers. The kids all cheered loudly. When they quieted down, she turned in her seat toward Frida. "You're not going to say anything to Grant, are you?"

"I told you I wasn't going to embarrass you. I just feel like getting out today, and I know Finn gets free tickets."

All the players did. They got a couple box seats and then a few general admission tickets. "I can ask if Finn gave all his tickets away."

"Awesome. Since I don't have any Storm shirts, should we make homemade Grant jerseys? You know

I've got all kinds of supplies at my house." Frida laughed loudly enough to get the attention of a nearby teacher.

Em gave them an apologetic smile for the disruption, before she glared at her friend. "Don't you dare."

She pouted. "Come on. You know I like any excuse to get dressed up."

It was true, all part of Frida's creative nature. "If I lend you one of Finn's jerseys, will you promise not to make a Grant shirt?"

"Of course. But I want the one you just won."

Em had spent a fortune on it and only worn it once. But lending it to Frida was a much better option than Frida wearing one with Vaughn on the back. She sighed. "Fine. I'll bring it when I pick you up."

"I DIDN'T KNOW this was the O'Brien cheering section," Miriam said as Frida and Em found their seats beside her, both wearing Finn's jerseys.

While Em wore an old one loose over her denim shorts for an easy casual look, Frida had taken a more creative approach to wearing hers. She tied the one-of-a-kind jersey at the waist and wore a black miniskirt that showed off her killer legs. The ensemble was topped off with homemade soccer earrings that dangled from her ears.

She looked like a sporty version of Ms. Frizzle without the bright, orange hair.

Being next to the boards, they were sure to be in a lot

of the live footage of the game and, as Miriam pointed out, they looked like a bunch of fangirls.

Though being accused of being part of her brother's cheering section was better than talking about her "crush" on Grant. Since Em would be sitting between the two women who had accused her of having a thing for Grant, she would gladly take the alternative.

She smiled at Miriam. "Maybe he's feeling left out after seeing the way you fawn all over Silas."

Miriam rolled her eyes. "Like I'm fawning over him. Silas has enough adoring fans that I don't need to feed his ego anymore."

Em lifted a brow.

"Exhibit A is sitting two rows behind me. Dark hair, Storm jersey, gorgeous. Even after Silas told her nothing was going to happen between them, she comes to all the games and screams his name the entire time."

Em made a show of reaching her arms above her head and spinning in both directions like she was stretching her back. When she turned around, she let her gaze go up to the stands behind them. Two rows up was a girl matching Miriam's description—though she wasn't nearly as pretty as Miriam had implied. "Does it bother you?"

Miriam shrugged. "It used to, but Silas made it obvious that he doesn't care about anyone else but me. It gets a little awkward at Storm events, but it's mostly just funny now."

That was good. Em was happy that Miriam was able to trust Silas after everything that had happened between them. She wondered what it must be like to be hurt so badly and forgive someone—more than that, love them.

Just then, the lights dimmed. The game was about to start.

The announcer called out the names of the Washington Orcas. There were a few scattered fans in the stands who'd made the trek to Florida to cheer on their team, but their clapping was barely audible. Em always felt bad for the visiting team. Not only were they fighting against the home field advantage, there were so few people cheering for them.

She started clapping as the rest of the Orcas ran onto the field. This earned her puzzling looks from both Miriam and Frida.

She shrugged. "What? I feel bad for them. Finn has told me how hard it is to be the visitor."

"Bleeding heart." Miriam bumped her shoulder. "As long as you cheer louder for the Storm."

She rolled her eyes. "Well, obviously."

Spotlights started moving across the stands. "Let's get ready to welcome your Florida Storm!"

The announcer's voice boomed through the arena, and Em snuck another glance back at Silas' super fan. She was jumping up and down and yelling through cupped hands.

"You really weren't kidding about that girl," she said to Miriam.

She gave Em a sly smile. "Just wait until he scores a goal."

Em giggled and turned her attention back to the field

where Storm players were called out one by one. She clapped and cheered for each one as they joined their teammates at midfield.

"Now for your starting lineup. Team captain and keeper, number one, Finn O'Brien!"

Em yelled as loudly as she could—loud enough to get her brother's attention. When he looked her way, she and Frida turned around to show him the back of their jerseys. Finn shook his head, but Em could see the ghost of a smile on his lips. He pretended to be embarrassed, but secretly loved the attention.

"On defense, number nine, Bastian Ramirez."

The girls continued to clap and cheer as he brought out some kids from the youth league to midfield with him.

"Also on defense, number seventy-seven, Vinny Nelson."

Em still clapped, though she knew her brother and "The Box" didn't have a great relationship. He was still part of the team, and she was going to support him.

"At midfield, number seven, Grant Vaughn."

He jogged onto the field in his green jersey. After stalking him online for the last week, she was surprised at how much more attractive he was in person. When he smiled up at the stands, her clapping hands stilled. When his eyes found hers, her breath caught in her chest.

As if he knew the effect he had on her, Grant's smile grew wider.

She pressed her lips together tightly to keep from smiling back, but Grant's gaze didn't move from Em. Not when the announcer called Silas and Cardosa out onto the field, not when a local singer sang the National Anthem, and not when both Miriam and Frida elbowed her in the ribs from either side.

The only thing that pulled Grant's attention from Em was the start of the game. He jerked his chin up at her just before he broke their eye contact and jogged over to his spot on the field.

Without him staring at her, Em felt like she could finally take a deep breath—though it was shaky as she released it.

"Oh, my goodness." Frida leaned in close. "It's worse than I thought."

Em's head jerked toward her best friend. "What do you mean?"

A sly grin touched Frida's lips. "That's not some silly little crush. You two were peering into each other's souls."

Em pushed Frida away from her. "Shut up."

"She's not wrong," Miriam said.

Em closed her eyes and groaned. *Great, did everyone have an opinion on what just happened?* "It was just a look."

"A meaningful one," Frida said.

Miriam nodded. "An intense one."

"A sensu—ow." Frida rubbed her arm, the arm that Em had punched. "I was just going to say—"

"I know what you were going to say, and I didn't come to watch the game tonight only to have you two team up against me."

"No, you came to watch Grant." Frida's voice was sing-songy as she said the midfielder's name.

Em's cheeks burned, and she wanted to sink down into her seat and hide from them both. She also knew that she'd be adding fuel to the fire if she did, so she straightened her back and turned her attention to the field.

The players from both teams waited for the referee to blow his whistle and start the game. They bounced on their toes to keep their muscles warm. Finn was lifting his knees and arms to keep everything loose.

When the whistle sounded, there was a flurry of movement in front of her. The Orcas had possession and drove the ball down the field toward the Storm's goal. Finn yelled at Vinny and Bastian to clear the ball out of there.

It was difficult to hear the words, even from her front-row seat, but his tone made it obvious that he wasn't happy that the ball was so close to him so early in the game.

The striker for Washington's team took a shot on goal. Finn jumped to the left to block the ball, barely getting up in time for the visiting team to take another shot. When the ball went flying at goal, Finn cleared it out to midfield.

The rest of the Storm players ran toward the other goal, and Cardosa got possession. He ran it upfield toward the Orca's keeper. He took the shot. Blocked.

"I forgot how fun these games are," Frida said. Her gaze was on the field, and she was leaning against the boards as the players ran by right in front of them.

So had Em before attending the previous week's game. She hated that she'd missed so many this season, and had already promised her brother that she'd make every effort to come to the rest of the home games to watch him play.

If that meant she got to watch Grant at the same time, there was no harm in that, was there?

Em had always been able to appreciate the way the guys played—Silas' shot record, Bastian's ability to stop the other team's forwards.

Now, she was impressed by Grant's energy. As the midfielder, he easily moved between the offensive and defensive roles. He knew when to shift the way he played and wasn't afraid of passing the ball to his teammates.

Em leaned against the boards as the players fought to get possession. Even though he didn't have the ball, her gaze went back to Grant. To her surprise, he was looking back at her. Even more surprising, Em liked that he was looking at her.

Yeah, she might be in trouble when it came to that boy, but at least she was going to enjoy it.

7

GRANT

GRANT MISSED the ball that Silas passed to him.

He'd been too busy looking over at Em—who looked absolutely gorgeous in her Storm jersey—and hadn't realized that the forward was kicking it back to him. A player from the other team got to the ball first and drove it down toward Finn.

Grant ran with the rest of the players behind the opposing team's player, but they weren't fast enough. When the forward took a shot, it went past Finn and into the net.

"Goal for Washington." The announcer's voice boomed through the arena, though it lacked enthusiasm and fell flat. The Storm was now losing to the other team by one point.

Grant wanted to kick himself for not paying attention. He let his team down, and even though Finn was the one who let the ball slip past, they'd made it difficult for their keeper by not being there to help guard the goal.

A strong hand slapped his back. Grant turned his head to see Silas standing there with a frown on his face. "Get your head in the game."

"I'm sorry. I don't know what came over me."

Silas' eyes flicked to the box seats next to the home bench—the seats where Em sat. "I think I do. And listen, I get it. I've gotten distracted by a pretty girl in the stands, but there are a lot of reasons why you don't want to go down that road."

Grant didn't ask Silas to elaborate. He knew the reasons he needed to keep his distance from Em. He'd been warned to keep away from Finn's sister by Bastian, and to keep away from fans in general from Finn.

He was already mad at himself for missing the ball, and he didn't want yet another lecture—not even from Silas, his mentor. It seemed like every guy on the team had an opinion about what Grant should and shouldn't be doing. He wasn't sure if it was because he was the rookie or if he had a sign on his back saying, "Please boss me around."

Regardless, he was pissed. "Noted," he said more gruffly than he intended before finding his spot on the field. The game was about to restart, and the ref had the ball in his hands at midfield.

When the whistle sounded, everyone started running around the field again. Grant was determined not to get distracted by Em or let his frustration with his teammates get in the way. He would play the best game he could, help the team win, and then he could think about everything else.

He followed the other players as they all moved upfield toward the other team's goal. Vinny passed Grant the ball, and since he was paying attention this time, he got it. Grant started dribbling the ball down the field.

An opposing player came up beside him and started pushing against him. Grant tried to shield the ball but with the pressure from the other guy, he ended up in an awkward position. His foot landed wrong and his ankle rolled under him.

Sharp pain shot through his ankle followed by a tingling sensation. He fell to the ground and immediately turned on his side. Most of the sounds around him faded away as he curled in on himself. He vaguely heard someone yelling that they had a player down.

I'm that player. I'm injured.

Grant could barely think straight through the pain, but he still tried to recall if there was a popping sound when his ankle rolled. If there was, it would mean the ligament had torn completely. An injury like that would put him out for the rest of the season. Even a partial tear would put him out longer than he wanted.

A fresh wave of pain pulled a small groan from him. He'd never had an injury like this before. He was so angry. Would his teammates be upset that he couldn't finish the game? Possibly the season?

Someone kneeled beside him, but Grant couldn't open his eyes. It hurt too much.

"Tell me what hurts." It was Mason, the team's athletic trainer.

"Ankle," he rasped.

"Can you turn on your back?"

"Yes," he said through gritted teeth. He twisted so that his back was against the turf and covered his eyes with his forearm.

"I'm going to touch your ankle, and it's going to hurt." Mason paused. "Ready?"

No, not really.

He nodded. When Mason moved his ankle, Grant bit his bottom lip to stop the cry that threatened to come out. The tangy taste of blood hit his lips as he tore through the tender skin, but any pain he might have felt in his mouth was eclipsed by what was going on with his foot.

"Stop," Grant managed to say.

Mason pulled his hands from his foot. "Okay. Do you need a stretcher, or can you walk off the field yourself?"

"No stretcher, but I can't do it by myself either."

"Of course."

He called Cardosa over to help as Grant shifted into a seated position. With a lot of help, Cardosa and Mason were able to get him up to his feet. Correction: foot. Grant bent his knee so his injured foot wouldn't touch the ground as he hopped on the other using the two men as crutches.

The arena erupted in cheers and clapping. He knew that they were happy to see him get up and off the field without having to be carried, but this didn't feel much better than that. He still needed help—and lots of it.

Once he was seated on the home bench, the game resumed. Not that Grant could focus on anything that was happening out there. Mason kept peppering him with questions and poking his ankle. Grant lifted his foot up on a chair and put ice on it.

"It's already bruising and swelling, but I don't think the ligament tore completely."

Thank goodness. Grant let out a sigh of relief.

"But I'm afraid it might be a grade two sprain."

He pressed his lips together forgetting how he'd cut the inside of his lip. He took a quick inhale at the sharp pain. "How long will I be out?"

Mason shrugged. "Depends. Maybe three to six weeks before you can play again."

"No." Grant's heart sunk and he shook his head. "I can't sit out for that long. It's too much of the season."

"The other option is to try to resume your normal activities now and make the tear worse. Maybe cause permanent damage. Want me to ask Coach what he thinks about that?"

Grant was surprised by his tone but, no matter how sarcastic the delivery, the message was clear. Grant needed to take his recovery seriously unless he wanted to stop playing soccer professionally sooner rather than later.

He rubbed his hands over his face and nodded. "Yeah, okay."

Mason's hand gripped the top of his shoulder. "I'm sorry. I hate to be the bearer of bad news. But you can be thankful it wasn't worse. A full tear would be several months."

Again, Mason was right, but that didn't make any of this easier. There was no way Grant would get Rookie of the Year at this point. He'd most definitely lose his spot in the starting lineup. He was just a name on the roster—completely useless.

He tried not to focus on that as he sat toward the back of the team's box while the game continued without him.

"Hey."

Em's voice pulled Grant from his pity-party. He looked from the field to where she stood, just on the other side of the board dividing their bench from fan seats. She gave him a small smile when his eyes met hers. Not only had he injured himself, but it was in front of the very girl he was trying to impress. "Hey."

"I'm not going to insult you by asking if you're okay."

Grant chuckled. That was the most obvious segue into talking about what had happened, but he still liked that she wasn't going to ask a question she already knew the answer to. "Thanks."

There was a small stretch of silence before she asked, "Did Mason say how bad it is?"

Grant's gaze went to his ankle where the ice pack still rested on it. "He thinks it's a grade two sprain. If he's right, I'll be out for several weeks."

"Oh, Grant. I'm so sorry."

He slowly nodded his head. "Yeah. It sucks."

"Want me to get you something? Since you can't play, you could always eat a greasy piece of pizza from the concession stand and make the other players jealous." She wiggled her eyebrows.

Grant laughed again. He loved that Em was trying to cheer him up when the situation was as bleak as it was, but he shook his head. There was no way he'd be able to keep anything down right now. "Maybe I could take a raincheck? We could grab some another time."

Her eyes widened slightly. "Like a date?"

"Your words, not mine. Not that I would call second-rate pizza a date." He shook his head. "What kind of guys do you let take you out?"

She looked away, and he wasn't sure if she'd answer or not. "The kind that thinks that counts."

He leaned over the best he could while having one of his legs propped up. "If you ever let me have the chance, I'd show you what it's like to go out on a real date."

She sighed. "Grant...I—"

Em didn't get to finish her thought because the ball was kicked out of play and was flying right toward her. Grant didn't think, he just reacted. He jumped up from his seat, letting his elevated leg fall as he leaned over the board and blocked the ball with his hands.

If he hadn't, the ball would have hit her in the side of her head. Sure, players hit headers all the time, but they were ready for it and used their foreheads. Getting hit on the side of the face without warning? It would hurt much worse.

Em gasped. "That was going to hit me."

The pain of moving his leg crashed over him, and he tried to keep his face neutral as he nodded. Grant didn't want to let on how badly it hurt to get up.

Her hand flew to her chest. "And your foot. You should have just yelled at me."

He shook his head. "And risked you turning your head and getting a broken nose or something? No way."

"But you must be in so much pain."

"It doesn't feel great." Grant eased back down onto his seat. "But it was worth it to make sure you weren't hurt."

Em's mouth fell open, and she looked like she was about to say something, but she closed her lips.

"Oh my goodness, Em!" her friend Frida cried from her other side.

Em looked at Grant, obviously hesitating like she wasn't sure if she should leave after he'd hurt himself.

"Go, let her fuss over you." He lifted a corner of his mouth, but inside he was disappointed. He'd love to be the one fussing right now. "I'm sure Mason is going to have a lot to say after my stunt anyway."

She bit her bottom lip and nodded. "Thank you, Grant."

"It was my pleasure."

8

EMMELINE

IT WAS MY PLEASURE.

Grant's words echoed in Em's mind as she hurried over to Frida and Miriam. As much as she wanted to stay with Grant, his adorable forwardness made it difficult to keep her walls up.

"Are you okay?" Frida's hands flew to Em's shoulders, her eyes wide. "That ball almost hit you in the head."

Em nodded. "Uh-huh."

"Thank goodness Grant was so fast! He just jumped off that chair to save you," Miriam said. The look of concern on her face matched Frida's.

"Yeah," Em said, her stomach in a tangle of knots.

"She might be in shock," Frida said. "Let's give her some space."

Em wasn't in shock, but she appreciated how Frida and Miriam both took a couple steps back.

"Do you need to sit down?" Miriam asked.

Em shook her head. She didn't get hit. She was fine—just a little confused.

She replayed the incident in her mind. It was just a stray ball. If it had hit her in the face, it would have hurt, but it wouldn't have been life-threatening. It definitely wouldn't have hurt more than the damage Grant had done to himself in his attempt to protect her.

And yet, he had said it was his pleasure.

With those words, it felt bigger than just stopping the ball from hitting her. Em wasn't sure if she was reading too much into it. Was she *trying* to find something that wasn't really there? After all, they didn't actually know each other outside of their Instagram flirtations. It wasn't like they were dating or anything.

Em snuck a glance in Grant's direction. His face contorted in pain as the athletic trainer manipulated his foot. Mason was speaking loud enough that Em could hear every word he said.

"What were you thinking?"

A muffled response from Grant.

"You need to stay off your foot until a doctor can take a look at it. And even then, you can't just jump up because you want to catch the ball."

Is that what Mason thought it was? Just an attempt for Grant to get to touch the ball even though he was injured—is that what everyone thought? It was possible they were all so focused on the game in front of them that they didn't realize Grant was being a hero—everyone but Frida and Miriam, of course, who had both freaked out.

Grant looked over at Em. His features softened when

his eyes met hers, and his lips curved into a small smile while Mason lectured him on the finer points of RICE—rest, ice, compression, and elevation.

Em's face burned under his gaze, and she glanced down at her feet. Her lips tipped up into a smile that matched his. When she looked back up, he was still looking at her.

"I'm sorry," she mouthed.

"Worth it," he mouthed back.

A shiver went through her.

Mason waved a hand in front of Grant's face. Following Grant's gaze, the athletic trainer glanced at Em and glared before his attention went back to his patient.

Someone cleared their throat. Em turned back to her friends.

Frida and Miriam both had smug expressions on their faces, and Em wondered when the two had become so in sync with one another. "What?"

Frida laughed before she gave Em an over-the-top look of innocence. "What?"

So that small exchange between her and Grant had not gone unnoticed. She bit her bottom lip.

"You've got it so bad," Frida said.

She shook her head. "I don't have anything. I was just looking over at Grant to make sure he was okay after what he did."

"Mm-hmm." Miriam gave Frida a sly look. "It's funny how the more you say you *don't* like Grant, the less I believe you."

Frida waggled her eyebrows suggestively. "Have you

seen the way they try to interact all sneaky on Instagram?"

"No." Miriam gasped. "What do they do?"

"They—"

"If I was trying to be *sneaky* about it, I would DM him instead," Em said. "But there's nothing to be private about since there's nothing going on." Her words had gotten progressively louder, and she glanced over to Grant to make sure he hadn't heard, though she wasn't entirely sure why. There *wasn't* anything going on. She was speaking the truth.

The coach was talking to him now. The stern look on his face made Em think that Mason wasn't the only one giving lectures.

"Don't worry," Miriam said. "He didn't hear you say there was nothing going on between you."

Frida giggled. "No trouble in paradise today."

Ugh. If she hadn't known Frida since they were kids, and if Miriam wasn't one of her only friends who loved the Storm as much as she did, Em would find new friends.

No, that wasn't true—not even close.

But that didn't mean she liked them teasing her about her non-crush on Grant.

"I just got a great idea," Miriam said, a wide smile on her face.

A pit formed in Em's stomach as the game went on forgotten. Whatever made Miriam look that gleeful was sure to be something that Em wouldn't like.

"So, you know how I'm the community outreach manager for the Storm, right?"

Em gave her a look that said "*duh.*"

"Well, Silas had this great idea earlier this season for some of the players to go visit local schools and read to the kids. Maybe it's because I haven't seen you all season, or maybe it's because there are so many elementary schools in the area—it's hard to remember them all—but I can't help but notice that they haven't visited *your* school."

The pit in Em's stomach got heavier. She sat down in one of the seats.

Meanwhile, Frida started clapping her hands in front of her. "Oh, I like where this is going."

"I was thinking this would be the perfect time for the guys to do another visit. And guess who likes going to community events."

"Silas?" Em deadpanned.

Miriam laughed. "Yeah, he does. But guess who else."

Em knew the answer Miriam was looking for, but refused to say his name out loud.

"I think she means Grant," Frida leaned down and whispered loudly.

Em smacked her leg. "I know who she meant."

"Good, then there won't be any surprises when he shows up to your classroom next week."

Next week? Em tried to ignore the way her heart thumped at the idea of seeing him outside of the arena.

. . .

TRUE TO MIRIAM'S WORD, the school set up a visit with the Storm players—though when the day came, only one was able to show up. It wasn't a surprise to Em that that player was none other than Grant Vaughn.

Em was just finishing a lesson on volcanoes when there was a knock on the door. She was surprised when Frida's face peaked through the crack when it opened.

"Sorry to interrupt, Ms. O'Brien. You have a visitor." She cleared her throat, though it sounded an awful lot like a stifled laugh. "Since I happened to be in the office when he arrived, I was happy to walk him to your classroom."

The visitor was obviously Grant, and even though she wasn't sure how Miriam and Frida had pulled it off, Em was sure that the timing of his visit during the art teacher's break was no coincidence.

Em struggled to keep her voice even. "Let him in."

Frida opened the door wider, and Grant soon entered the classroom hunched over a pair of crutches wearing a small backpack. Even though he'd confirmed his sprain on social media, she'd almost forgotten he'd injured himself at the game. She hated seeing him like that. He was fit and...a guest in her classroom.

This wasn't the time to ogle him. She smiled at him as he slowly made his way to the front of the classroom. Thankfully, her students were all too young to notice the way her cheeks got redder the closer he got. She fought against the urge to fan her face as he stopped beside her.

"Thanks for coming today."

"It's my pleasure."

My pleasure. There were those pesky words again. They had the same effect on her as the first time he'd spoken them, and now she really wanted to fan her cheeks.

She focused on her students instead. "Class, we have a special visitor today. This is Grant Vaughn. He's a player for the Storm."

A hand immediately went up. Em pointed to the boy in the middle of the room. "Yes?"

"What's the Storm?"

Em turned to Grant. "That's a great question. Would you like to answer that for him, Mr. Vaughn?"

He gave her a quizzical look. Non-teachers—especially younger adults—who came to her class always seemed put off by formal introductions. But rather than let him dwell on it, she gave him an encouraging nod.

Grant adjusted his weight over the crutches. "The Storm is a professional arena soccer team based here in Waterfront."

Another student raised their hand. Grant called on him. "You have a question?"

"What's arena soccer?"

Em stood back as he started describing the sport. It was short, engaging, and completely age-appropriate. Em was pleasantly surprised; not everyone knew how to talk to kids. When he was done with his spiel, he swung the black backpack from his back so that it was in front of him. With some careful maneuvering, he unzipped it and pulled out a stack of tickets. "And if you're really good while I read, I promise to leave some free tickets with your teacher. Sound good?"

Excited chatter went through the class.

"The games are a lot of fun. And you know what the best part is?" Grant said. The room quieted. "Ms. O'Brien is a big soccer fan, and you'll probably get to see her if you go."

Em's kids were nine and ten. They were at an age where some of them still loved seeing teachers outside of school, while others were getting too cool for things like that. The mix of expressions showed the clear division of the students.

Not missing a beat, he turned to Em and asked, "Did she tell you how I protected her at the last game?"

She wanted to cover her face with her hands, but as their teacher, she needed to have some level of decorum. Em plastered a smile on her face and said through slightly gritted teeth, "As a matter of fact, I didn't."

"Then I should tell it."

The kids all leaned forward as one of the girls asked if that was why he was on crutches.

"That would be really cool, but no. I hurt my foot playing soccer." Grant let out a good-natured chuckle. "I saved your teacher from a ball that flew into the stands."

"The balls go into the stands?" another kid asked.

"Sometimes, and people can get really hurt if they get hit. Thankfully, I was there to make sure your teacher didn't come to school with a giant bruise on her face."

There was more chatter between the students,

though it seemed like the majority of them were impressed.

Em wasn't sure if she wanted to scream at Grant for being so charming or change her no-dating-players rule on the spot for the very same reasons. She stepped forward. "Arena soccer is very fun. And like Mr. Vaughn said, I enjoy going to the games. But he didn't just come in to tell you stories about the Storm. He came to read a few books as well."

Some of the kids who enjoyed hearing about sports instead of reading books groaned, but she gave them her best do-not-question-me-unless-you-want-to-go-to-the-office look. It wasn't a look Em used often, only when she needed her students to know that she was serious.

When they settled, Em grabbed a chair for Grant to sit in. The smile he gave her in return melted her heart. He slowly eased into the seat and pulled a couple books out of his bag. They were the typical books kids this age enjoyed, and Em recognized all of them but one. It looked much older than the rest and had a very plain cover.

Grant started with the unknown book. "This was one of my favorite books growing up. It's called *Red Riding: A Story of How Katy Tells Tony a Story Because It Is Raining.*"

That was one heck of a title, but Em was intrigued.

"I have an older sister who was quite bossy when we were kids—still is. Our mom used to read us this book because she said Katy and Tony reminded her of us." He lifted the book and started reading.

The book was as silly as the title. It was a rainy day, so the older sister decided to tell her younger brother the tale of *Little Red Riding Hood*. It was sweet because the younger brother kept interrupting the older sister, and she kept correcting him in return.

Em found herself laughing on more than one occasion and tried to imagine younger Grant as the precocious boy from the story. She shook her head. Nope, that wasn't a good idea at all. If she imagined Grant as that sweet boy, she might be tempted to think he was a sweet guy. And no matter how wonderful he seemed now, Em knew that those first impressions could be deceiving.

So could the second and third and fourth.

She was thankful when Grant was done sharing that adorable book from his childhood and started reading something less personal. It was a book about monsters written by the latest celebrity turned children's author.

The entire time, the kids listened quietly and were respectful. And Em couldn't help the pull she felt toward the man reading to them.

9

GRANT

GRANT LOVED READING to the kids.

After being completely useless for the past few days, it was nice to feel like he was making a difference. Ever since his injury, he wasn't able to participate in practices, though he still attended, and all of his workouts were modified. Grant wasn't even allowed to dress out for the next few games. If it wasn't for the fact that he lived with other players, he wouldn't feel like he was a part of the team at all.

Getting to go to a school in a Storm shirt with a stack of tickets was just what he needed. Seeing Em was a bonus.

He finished reading the last story to the class and looked up at her for direction. He wasn't sure if he should go back to telling soccer stories, pass out tickets, or leave. He didn't want to leave.

Em looked up at the clock on the wall before she walked over next to Grant. His heart raced as she got closer. Unaware of her effect on him, Em addressed her students. "We've got about five minutes until lunch. Grab your lunch box if you have one, and we'll line up and go down to the cafeteria a little early."

The sound of talking and chairs scraping the floor soon filled the silence. Grant smiled and leaned over toward Em. "Breaking the rules in front of all these impressionable children. How do you sleep at night?"

Don't think about that, Grant.

"I'm the teacher, I make the rules." She winked playfully in his direction.

He leaned over and picked up his bag. "Should I leave the tickets on your desk?"

"Oh, right." She reached out and took them from him. Her fingers brushed up against his, causing his heart to beat faster.

Leaning against his crutch, he hitched his thumb at the door where the kids were lined up and waiting for their teacher. "Well, I guess I'd better get going."

Em bit her bottom lip. Too soft for her students to hear, she said, "If you're hungry, you can stay and eat with the class."

He would have loved that, but there was a small problem. "I didn't bring any cash, and I have a feeling the lunch ladies don't accept American Express."

She smiled. "I have enough money in my account that I can treat you to a four-dollar meal. Hope you like corn dogs and baked fries."

"If I didn't know better, I'd say you were asking me on a lunch date."

Of course, he *did* know better. Em didn't date players—a fact she made abundantly clear every time they talked.

"I wouldn't consider corn dogs anything special. Trust me, if we ever went on a real date, you'd know it."

Grant laughed at the way she stole the words he'd used about arena pizza. "I'd be happy to stay for this non-date lunch."

Em smiled at him once more before telling the line leader to start walking toward the cafeteria. Her students were quiet and orderly as they walked down the halls. Was she the kind of teacher who ruled with an iron fist? Grant didn't think so; she was too playful, too sweet.

"I usually eat in the teacher's lounge since we have staff members that monitor lunches, but I think the kids would love it if you ate in the cafeteria."

"Will you be in there?"

"Or course. I wouldn't just throw you to the wolves like that."

"It's good to know you've got my back," he said, swinging his good foot in front of him for another step. He hated that he still wasn't completely steady on his crutches and hoped Em didn't notice.

"Don't get too excited, it gets really loud in there."

"And Storm games don't?"

"Good point."

Grant kept stealing glances at Em as they walked toward the cafeteria. How was it possible that she kept getting more beautiful every time he saw her? He debated telling her that as the students filed through the doors before them but lost his chance when another adult joined them.

It was Frida, and she had a sly smile on her face. Her voice had a sing-song quality to it as she greeted them. "How's it going?"

A blush creeped up Em's neck.

Interesting.

"Just fine. Why aren't you in the teacher's lounge, Ms. Hall?" she said through clenched teeth.

"Oh? So, I'm Ms. Hall now?"

"You're right, you're acting childish, so I definitely shouldn't call you that."

Frida stuck her tongue out and earned an eye roll from Em.

Grant couldn't help but laugh at their interaction. It reminded him so much of his relationship with his sister.

"You are not allowed to laugh, Mr. Vaughn."

Grant wiggled his eyebrows at Frida. "Looks like I still get to keep my grownup title."

Em glared at him, though the twitch of her mouth softened it. "You know what? Just for that, I should let Frida babysit you and go enjoy a quiet lunch in the teachers' lounge—by myself."

"No," Grant and Frida said in unison.

Em's eyes went back and forth between them. "Now I'm thinking I definitely need to go do that."

Frida put her arm over Em's shoulders. "If anyone is going to the teachers' lounge, it's me. I'm just not cut out for the lunchroom. But enjoy your *yummy* lunch for me."

Grant's pulse picked up at the look shared between

the two women. When Em's blush returned, the warm rush of victory flooded into him: *he* was the yummy.

Even though Frida had to know all about Em's no-dating-players rule, he couldn't help but enjoy knowing that he could get Em all flustered. It was only fair since she had the same effect on him.

"I'll see you guys later," Frida said with a small wave over her shoulder and left.

Once she was gone, the line seemed to move impossibly slower, and without Frida as a buffer between them, Grant was suddenly unsure of how to act with Em.

"I want to thank you again for stopping that ball."

Grant released a breath, thankful she'd broken the awkward silence between them. "You're welcome."

"I'm glad you got to look like a hero in front of the kids today." She grabbed both their trays. "But I hate that you might have made your ankle worse."

"I'm out for the next few games, regardless. I told you, I was happy to do it."

"Well, thank you...again."

"You're welcome...again." His smile was teasing, but the one she returned was full of warmth that spread through his body.

When they'd made it through the line, Grant followed Em to a table. He knew they were eating in the cafeteria to spend time with the kids, but he was still surprised when Em plopped their trays right in the middle of a long table filled with third graders. At least they were sitting next to each other.

With some careful maneuvering, he sat down on the

stiff plastic bench. A dozen pairs of eyes were on him instantly. And almost as quickly, the questions started coming from all directions. The kids all wanted to know what position he played, how long he'd been playing, how much he made—he didn't answer that one—what his favorite music was, and so on.

He barely got a bite in with the constant barrage of questions, but he enjoyed every minute—even more than reading to them. Despite his injury, the kids treated him like a celebrity athlete. It was exactly the boost he needed to lift the sadness of being out for a few games.

When he looked over at Em, he caught a satisfied smile on her lips. Did she know this would happen and how much it would mean? Already, he was having a hard time not falling for her.

AN HOUR LATER, after finishing up his non-date lunch and driving home, he pulled out his laptop to video chat with his sister. Between seeing Em and Frida tease each other in the cafeteria, and reading his favorite childhood book to Em's class, he realized that he really missed Katherine.

The two had been good about texting and interacting online, but he couldn't remember the last time he sat down just to catch up. When her smiling face appeared on the screen, he instantly felt homesick.

"Hey, Granty Panty."

Grant groaned. Okay, maybe he wasn't *that* homesick. He could go the rest of his life without hearing the ridiculous nickname his sister had given him when they were little. Every year, a small part of him hoped that Katherine would eventually stop calling him that, but Grant would always be her kid brother. They could be old and gray at his niece's wedding, and he'd still be Granty Panty.

She lifted her brows. "And to think, it only took a severe injury that put you out of commission to call me."

"Yeah, I miss you too." He really did.

Katherine asked him how his school visit had gone, and when Grant had finished telling her about it, she leaned forward so that her face filled more of the screen.

"And is *Emmeline* madly in love with you yet?"

Grant laughed. "I've told you, it's not like that."

"Yes, but I've also known you your entire life. I've never seen you light up like this when you've talked about a girl."

"Note to self: no more video chats."

She rolled her eyes. "You act like I didn't already know before seeing your love-sick expression whenever you say her name."

"I can still hit 'end call.'"

Katherine leaned back in her seat. "You could, but you won't."

"Oh yeah?"

His sister shrugged. "You haven't seen your nieces yet. It would break their hearts not to say hi."

Grant felt a pang of guilt. Between family dinners with his parents, and babysitting so that his sister and her husband could go out on Friday nights, he was used to seeing his nieces several times a week. Now that he was states away, he missed his uncle role. "You're right."

"Plus, I think you want to talk more about your girlfriend."

"She's not my girlfriend."

"But you want her to be."

Grant closed his eyes and sighed. Dating Em sounded great on paper, but every time he gave it any more than a superficial thought, it didn't seem like a good idea.

First, there was the issue of the O'Brien siblings. Em kept insisting that she didn't date players, and Finn had a strict no-dating-my-sister rule. But if that wasn't enough, there was the fact that Grant didn't live in Florida—not permanently. He lived in a team house with no roots in Waterfront. When the season was over, he'd move back to his apartment in Kansas City. Em had a teaching career here in town, and eventually Grant would pursue his own career...once he figured out what it was.

"Katherine, you know I like her. She's gorgeous and funny and—"

"So what's the problem?"

He ran a hand over his face. "It's complicated."

"Can I give you some sisterly advice?"

"Are you going to take no for an answer?"

"Obviously not." She laughed. "But if you really like this girl, and it sounds like she likes you too, maybe you should explore what could happen between you. If it's love, you can figure out the rest. Just like I did with Joseph."

"Not everyone is willing to move cross-country for someone."

She smiled. "But they are for the right one. Just something to think about."

Grant would think about it, but he wasn't the one who needed convincing. He was willing to give things a shot as soon as Em gave him the green light.

"Can we come in yet?" said a young girl's voice from the screen.

"Please, Mommy," said another. "We want to see Uncle Grant."

Katherine laughed. "I don't think I'm going to keep them out much longer. So if you have anything else you want to get off your chest, do it now or forever hold your peace."

Grant was relieved for his nieces' interruption. He didn't think that he could talk relationships with his sister much longer. "Let them in."

Katherine called the girls, and they came running in. They basically pushed their mom out of the way to fill the entire screen of his laptop. They started long monologues about their toys, their friends, and how much they missed him.

After fifteen minutes of this, Grant finally got to speak. "I miss you guys too."

It was true. He did.

But this was finally his chance to do what he loved for a bit.

And maybe find love too.

10

EMMELINE

SOMETHING FELT off to Em at Saturday night's Storm game.

Normally, it was all about cheering for her brother and the other guys while eating greasy concession food with Miriam.

But this week, she couldn't stop thinking about Grant. He invaded her thoughts without permission, and as much as she had tried to deny it, she had a crush on him—not that she was willing to admit it to Frida.

Her friend walked beside her as they entered the arena. Em hadn't planned on inviting her after she'd not-so subtly played matchmaker at the school, but Frida had begged until Em said yes.

They wore matching O'Brien jerseys, just as they had the week before. Miriam was already there when they got to their seats, typing wildly on her phone. When she was done, she looked up at Em, eyes wide. "Thank goodness you're here."

Em raised her brows. "I didn't realize my attendance was so important."

"It's not. I mean, it is." Miriam closed her eyes and took a deep breath. "I have this really fun halftime show planned for tonight's game, but I absolutely cannot use one of the people Greg chose to participate."

It wasn't uncommon for the Storm office staff to put together halftime shows that involved fans. Sometimes it was a shooting contest to win free tickets, or a trivia question for a gift card from a corporate sponsor. One time, they sold ping-pong balls to fans for a chance to win a brand-new car. They pulled the vehicle onto the field, opened the sunroof, and let everyone throw their balls from the stands. If they got a ball in, they won the car.

But Em couldn't think of any reason to bar someone from participating in any of those events. What did Miriam have cooking this time?

"Uh..."

"Did you see the sign-up online?"

Em shook her head. "No. Why?" Other than a quick peek at Grant's Instagram, she had been swamped at work with much less time than usual for time scrolling through social media this week. Good for convincing herself her crush was under control, bad for keeping up to date on Storm news.

"So, Greg and I thought it would be fun to host a *The Dating Game* spoof during halftime featuring one of the players."

Frida laughed.

Em tried to, but the laugh got stuck in her throat. The

words "dating" and "players" gave her a bad feeling about the direction this was headed.

"We had a sign-up where anyone who wanted to play could sign up online. The only requirements were agreeing to be at the game in case your name was chosen and to be willing to go down on the field during halftime. There were a ton of entries, and Greg picked three names. Two of them seem fine, but the third..." Miriam's eyes darted up into the stands.

"What's wrong with the third?" Frida asked, lowering her voice and leaning forward in her seat.

"The third is a woman named McKensie. She's the fan who used to stalk Silas."

Em remembered Miriam pointing her out at another game. "Silas agreed to be the bachelor for *The Dating Game*?" Em asked incredulously.

Miriam shook her head. "Oh, no. We're not using any of the uniformed players. They'll be in the locker room with Coach. But I don't want to subject *any* of our players to this chick. She's legit crazy."

A sense of dread pooled in Em's stomach. "Who's the player?"

"No one is supposed to know before the halftime show—definitely not the bachelorettes. And please know that I'm not asking because—"

"It's Grant, isn't it?" Frida squealed. "This is so perfect."

Miriam bit her bottom lip. "I know we've teased you about having a crush on Grant, and I swear this wasn't some elaborate plan."

Memories of the school visit came to Em's mind. "You mean like having Grant show up during Frida's break."

Miriam looked down at her fingernails while Frida sniggered.

Em folded her arms across her chest and huffed. "I knew you two were in cahoots."

"But this is different." Miriam put her hands out. "Originally, I had planned on having Barros do it, but then Grant got injured and Greg picked McKensie, of all people. Since I don't have the list of names of everyone who entered, I've got to improvise."

"Why not Frida?"

Her traitorous friend shook her head. "I'm not going down there. I get nervous in the spotlight."

Em snorted. That was a lie if she'd ever heard one.

"Please, Em?" Miriam asked, raising her hands and putting on massive puppy dog eyes. "I'd owe you big time."

Em bit her lip. *The Dating Game* wasn't technically dating, and she liked to help Miriam with Storm events when she could. "What would I have to do?"

Miriam's face lit up. "It's super simple. At halftime, Grant will walk out to midfield. We're going to put a partition up and then introduce all three contestants. You'll be on the other side where he can't see you. He's going to ask everyone three questions, and you just need to answer them. When he's done, he'll choose one lucky lady to spend the rest of the game with in the VIP section."

"I already have great seats," Em said.

"Well, for *most* people it's an upgrade. Besides, it'll be over there." Miriam pointed to one of the corners of the arena. Behind the plexiglass near the goal was a small table with roses in the center.

Em groaned. "So, it's like a *date*, date."

"Well, you'll be watched by tons of people, including your brother, plus Greg wouldn't let me serve champagne since one of the contestants is twenty, so you'll have to settle for sparkling grape juice." She shrugged. "But yeah, it's a date."

Em had completely forgotten about Finn. Nothing like your brother watching you talk to the guy you liked. That added an extra element of uncomfortableness to the entire situation. "I don't know."

Miriam sighed loudly and threw up her hands. "Okay, let me go tell McKensie she'll be doing it. How do you think Grant feels about random girls tattooing his name on their chest?"

A sudden blaze of jealousy shot through Em. Sure, it was just a teeny crush, and Miriam was most likely exaggerating, but that didn't mean she liked the thought of Grant being forced to spend the whole second half with a super-hot, super fan. She closed her eyes and blurted, "Fine, I'll do it," before she could change her mind.

Miriam leaned across Frida to wrap her arms around Em. "Thank you, thank you, thank you. I was cutting it close. You have no idea how freaked out I was about this."

"Oh, I think I have a pretty good idea." She had roughly an hour before she was supposed to go down on the field and compete against other women for a chance to win Grant's heart...or at least, an hour of his time.

It should've been simple enough, but now that she'd admitted her crush to herself, she was going to have a hard time acting casual about it.

"We should probably get you cleaned up," Frida said.

Em looked down at her outfit—she'd paired Finn's jersey with a pair of skinny jeans that night—and touched her hair. "What do you mean?"

"It's *The Dating Game*. You should look like you're about to go on a date."

Em snapped her fingers. "Silly me. I forgot to bring my spare dress tonight, and I'm not running home to get it."

Frida rolled her eyes. "I just meant I could give you a more dramatic makeup look."

Why did Frida assume Em had any of that with her? "I don't have my makeup either."

Frida lifted her purse. "Luckily, I do. And I'd love to do something with your hair."

"There's nothing wrong with my hair." She glanced over at Miriam who suddenly found the board between them and the field *very* interesting. She turned back to Frida. "You've got ten minutes before the game starts."

Frida nodded. "Deal."

IT TOOK Frida twenty minutes to do Em's makeup and hair in the arena's public bathroom, and as much as she didn't want to admit it, Em was thankful for her best friend's magic touch. So much so, she didn't mind that they missed the beginning of the game.

She couldn't change her outfit, and worried about looking silly after having her hair and makeup done while still wearing a Storm jersey, but Frida was, after all, an artist. When Em was finally allowed to see herself in the mirror, she couldn't believe how amazing she looked.

Her eyeshadow was darker, but not too sultry, her cheeks had just a touch of pink to them—which would hopefully cover any unwelcome blushes—and her lips were bright red. As for her hair, Frida had pulled half of it up into a soft, romantic style.

Unfortunately, the first date jitters were hitting hard, and Em fought the urge to touch her hair or face during the second quarter. Her stomach fluttered with a million butterflies, and her breathing got shallower with every minute they got closer to halftime.

It's not a real date.

He might not even choose you.

The thought of Grant spending an hour at that romantic table with another woman hurt more than she thought it would, which only made her nerves go back into overdrive. She struggled to pay attention to the game unfolding in front of her, and by the time the buzzer signifying the end of the first half sounded through the arena, Em was seriously considering bailing altogether.

"Come on, let's go," Miriam said and began walking around the outside of the arena toward one of the goals. Em had no choice but to follow.

Looks like I missed that boat.

There were two other women standing there waiting. They both looked like they were in their mid-twenties, and just as suspected, they were gorgeous. One of them wore an over-the-top pink, frilly dress, and the other wore jeans just like Em, but instead of a jersey, she had on a low-cut top that left little to the imagination.

Miriam walked over and introduced herself while the arena staff rolled up the net. Greg and some other Storm staff members brought the partition and chairs out to the field.

"I'm going to walk out on the field and play host in just a minute. When I call your name, I want you to walk out onto the field and sit down in one of the chairs." Miriam grabbed three microphones off a nearby table. "When you sit down, press the button on the side. When you do, your mic is live."

Em's hands were shaking so much she nearly dropped hers when Miriam handed it to her.

"Grant Vaughn is our bachelor tonight. Greg is leading him onto the field from the other direction so he won't see you. His choice will be based strictly on your answers. They're silly questions, so don't stress. Remember to smile and have fun." Miriam winked at Em before she turned and walked out onto the field.

Once she was out there, she introduced herself and the bachelor. Then she explained the rules of the game.

The woman in the pink dress looked at Em. She smiled timidly. "Are you nervous?"

Yes!

Em shook her head. "Not really. I think it'll be fun."

"Grant is super cute," revealing t-shirt woman said. "I wonder what the odds of getting a second date are if we win tonight?"

Hopefully zero if you win.

Em instantly felt guilty for the thought. Clearly neither of them had a no-dating-soccer-players rule. Grant should spend his time and attention on someone who could return it fully, not someone who'd only crush in secret and do nothing about it. "I think this is just for fun," she said to the woman.

T-shirt woman laughed. "Well, yeah. But I plan to take advantage of my time with him if I get the chance."

"Oh, they just called my name," pink dress woman said. She took a deep breath and walked out onto the field. When she reached the chairs, she sat down.

Miriam called t-shirt woman. She sauntered onto the field oozing confidence.

Em wiped her hands on her jeans. When Miriam finally called her name, Em plastered a smile on her face and walked out. She took her seat next to the other two women.

"Let's give our contestants a round of applause." Holding her own microphone, Miriam clapped her hands. When the applause died down, she turned to the three women. "Before we get to our questions, I'd love for y'all to introduce yourselves to our bachelor. Without saying your name, give him your best hello."

Contestant number one held up her microphone. "Um, hello?"

Grant chuckled. "Hi, it's nice to meet you."

Contestant number two held up her microphone. In a deep, sexy voice, she said, "Hello."

Grant cleared his throat. "Hello."

It was Em's turn. She held up her microphone. "Hi, Grant."

Unlike the previous two introductions, hers was met with silence.

11

GRANT

"HI, GRANT."

His pulse went from zero to sixty with those two words. He knew that voice. Suddenly the game he'd never wanted to play in the first place just got a whole lot better.

When Miriam had first approached him to be the bachelor in the team's version of *The Dating Game,* he was slightly annoyed. He knew the only reason she'd asked him was because he wouldn't be able to play in the game. If he was able to dress out in his uniform, he never would have been considered.

Not only that, he knew Em would be watching the game. He hated the idea of her having front row seats to the halftime show that included him interviewing three women and then going on a fake date for the second half.

Miriam had assured him it was supposed to be something fun and silly. He'd agreed in the end since it was a way to show his commitment to the team even when he couldn't be on the field.

So, he'd put on his best suit and hung out in the VIP section dreading the halftime show. If he'd known Emmeline was going to be one of the contestants, he would have volunteered the second Miriam had mentioned it.

"Well, contestant number three, it looks like you've rendered our bachelor speechless," Miriam said into her microphone. The fans laughed in response.

Grant lifted his mic to his mouth and tried to keep the excitement out of his voice. "Nice to meet you contestant three."

Miriam pressed her lips together, fighting a smile. "Now that we've gone through our introductions, I'll let our lucky bachelor ask his questions."

Grant looked down at the note cards in his lap. Miriam had given him a stack of ten cards, each with a question on it, and told him to pick his top three. Grant hadn't even looked through them since he wasn't actually looking to find love.

He read the top one. "If you could travel anywhere in the world, where would it be and why?"

"I would love to go to Paris," the first contestant said with a soft, dreamy voice. "It's the city of love."

Grant would have also loved to go to Paris someday, but it was the kind of generic answer that said nothing about the person giving it. "Contestant number two?"

"I would love to go to Hawaii," she said, her voice as sultry as before. "Because I look amazing in a bikini and would spend a lot of time on the beach."

There were a few whistles from the crowd. She was really laying it on thick. Only the first question, and he was already afraid that if he chose her, she'd be trying to rip his shirt off during their "date."

He shuddered. "Contestant number three?"

"I think I'd go to Kansas City. I hear some pretty cool people live there."

Grant could hear the smile in her voice. For a moment, he wondered how she knew where he was from, but remembered they'd spent a lot of time liking each other's posts on Instagram. She knew he was from Kansas City, the same way he knew that she'd gone to University of Florida and was a Gator through and through.

He liked that they knew these things about each other. With a smile on his face, he looked down at the next question. "What's your favorite food?"

"I like pizza." Another standard answer.

"Yum, I do too," he said. "Contestant number two?"

"Chocolate covered strawberries."

Grant had to press his lips together to stop the laugh that threatened to come to the surface. "Contestant number three?"

"I could eat tacos every single day. There's this truck that has the best tacos in town."

She liked tacos from a truck? He wondered which ones were her favorite and made a mental note to ask her later which truck it was—and then offer to take her. He could barely wait to see her.

Excited to finish the game so he could spend time with her, he read the next question. "If you were a musical instrument, what sound would you make?" His face immediately scrunched up.

What kind of question is that?

There was a longer-than-usual pause between the question and the first contestant's answer. Eventually, she started beatboxing—poorly.

"Contestant two?"

Clearly as thrown off by the question as the first woman, Miss SexyPants also started beatboxing.

"Contestant number three?"

Grant waited for yet another rendition of a drum set and was surprised when Em started making a terrible screeching sound into the microphone. He barely resisted the urge to cover his ears.

"I'm a violin," she said once everyone in the arena had stopped laughing.

Yep, it was official. He was into her before but now he was a total goner.

"Well, that was enlightening," Miriam said, taking control again. "Grant, you've got three lovely ladies to choose from. You'd be lucky to spend time with any of them in our VIP section. So, who is it going to be?"

Fans started calling out numbers. Some held up fingers to indicate which girl he should pick. He saw an awful lot of twos, mostly from the men. Not that it mattered, he knew who he would choose already. "I'd like to go on a date with contestant number three."

The fans cheered.

"Well, before you meet your date for the rest of

tonight's game, let's meet the women you didn't choose. Contestant number one."

A woman wearing a hot pink dress walked around the partition. She was pretty, but not Em. He stood up with the help of his crutches and gave her an awkward hug before she walked off the field.

"Contestant number two."

A woman wearing jeans and a tee walked into view. The shirt was just as tight and low as Grant expected. He also gave her a quick hug before she walked off the field, though she held on a bit after he'd let go.

"And contestant number three, your special date in the VIP section for the rest of tonight's game, Emmeline O'Brien."

Grant couldn't stop the wide grin as she walked around the corner. He was happy to see her expression mirrored his own. He put his arm out waiting for her hug and held his breath when she hesitated.

After what felt like an eternity, she walked to him and let him wrap his arm around her. "I knew it was you," he whispered near her ear.

She shivered.

When he pulled back, he jerked his head over to the table set up for their date. "Shall we?"

"We shall."

They walked off the field and the Storm office and arena staff grabbed the chairs and partition. In no time, the field was ready for gameplay again, and not a moment too soon. The players were returning from the locker room. They passed by them as they walked to the VIP section.

Bastian's lips turned down into a frown after his gaze passed between Grant and Em. He slowed down and opened his mouth like he was going to say something but shook his head and kept walking.

A couple other guys, including Silas, gave him wide-eyed looks as they passed.

When Finn got close, his brows lowered, but he didn't look angry. Confused, maybe?

It didn't matter. Not now.

All that mattered was him and Em and the next hour they got to spend together. It might be the only chance he got to convince Em to date him.

Grant planned to make the most of this opportunity.

12

EMMELINE

EM TRIED to ignore the look Finn gave her as they passed each other on the field.

He knew her no-dating-players rule better than anyone else.

When Travis destroyed her trust in men in high school, Finn had quickly become the only guy she trusted. Not only had he beat the crap out of Travis, earning him a week-long suspension, his reputation had protected Em the rest of her high school days.

When Mark had done something similar in college, Finn hadn't been around to teach him a lesson, which was good since there would have been legal repercussions since he wasn't a juvenile anymore, but he'd been there to listen to her as she vowed off men forever.

He was the only family she had, and he always looked out for her. Always.

So she knew he had to be confused about her walking off the field with Grant. She'd make sure to explain everything after the game. It was a silly thing to help Miriam. Grant wasn't like Travis or Mark. He wasn't even like Damien, who Finn used to play with on the Storm.

But she'd deal with that later. For now, she was going to enjoy the next hour pretending the VIP section of the arena was a special date.

When Grant and Em arrived at the high-top table decorated for their date, a waitress in a long, black dress approached them with a large glass bottle. She bowed at the waist. "Good evening. Can I start you off with some sparkling grape juice?"

Oh, yeah. This is going to be cheesy.

At least Grant didn't check out the other woman's cleavage when she bent over.

Miriam had told her that they weren't serving alcohol as part of the date, but surely she could buy some on her own dime since the arena had a bar? She looked up at the waitress. "Can I get champagne instead?"

The waitress' facade faltered. "It's not included in the date. And I think we only have white wine."

"That's totally fine."

The waitress turned to Grant. "And you, sir?"

"I'll have a beer."

"Of course." She looked down at the untouched bottle in her hands. "I wonder what I should do with this."

Em pointed to the box seats where Miriam and Frida still sat. "I'm sure those two ladies would love to drink it. The blonde is the lady who set up *The Dating Game* in the first place."

The waitress smiled and nodded. "Okay. I'll be back with your drinks in a minute."

Once she was gone, Em looked over at Grant. For the first time since the big reveal, she got to get a good look at him. His blond hair was combed back from his face giving her a better view of his blue eyes. He wore a gray suit that hugged his muscular frame—and covered his tattoos.

"You look really nice tonight," she said, barely resisting the urge to tell him to take off the coat jacket and push his sleeves up.

What is wrong with you?

His mouth curved into a wide grin. "Thank you. You do, too, though I feel a little strange knowing you're wearing another man's jersey."

Em giggled. "It's my *brother's*. You know that. And besides, it just so happens to be my last name too."

He leaned forward. "Still, I wish it was my name on it."

A shiver ran through her at Grant's deep voice. She fought against her trembling and forced her voice into a light tone. "Well, if you're so worried about it, you could just give me one of yours."

"Is that all it takes?" His face lit up, and she almost laughed at how easy it was to make him happy. "Since this is my first year playing professionally, I've only got the two game day jerseys, but I'll happily lend you my away jersey anytime we play a home game."

"I couldn't. I'd be too afraid something would happen to it."

"I know you'd take good care of it. And it would give me an excuse to see you after our date, which is already going better than I thought it would."

"Tell me about it. It's way better than my last date with a Storm player." She clamped her lips shut. She hadn't meant to say that out loud.

"Wait, I thought you didn't date Storm players?"

Em's face heated. It was so embarrassing to admit, and she'd already made a fool of herself tonight—in front of all the fans. She wasn't ready to rehash her disaster with Damien just yet. "That's a story for another time."

"Another time?" He leaned forward. "All I'm hearing is excuses to go out on another date when we've barely started our third."

"Third? What are you talking about?" She rested her elbow on the table and leaned forward. "This is our first date, and that's assuming this even counts as a real date."

The waitress reappeared and put their drinks on the table next to the roses.

"It absolutely counts," he said when the waitress walked off again. A corner of his mouth lifted into a teasing smile. "And it's date number three."

"How do you figure that?" She raised her brows.

He lifted a single finger. "Well, after I saved your life, you stood me up for pizza."

Em laughed. Every time Grant told the story of the soccer ball, it got more elaborate. In a couple weeks, she was sure the soccer ball was going to turn into a bomb that Grant somehow diffused with his eyes closed. "Okay."

He lifted a second finger. "Then you bought me lunch on our second date."

"I told you, that wasn't a real date. Cafeteria food doesn't count."

"Debatable." He shrugged. "Which makes this date three. You keep *saying* you're not interested in dating me, but somehow you ended up on that field anyway. How much did you have to pay Miriam to get there?"

Em shook her head, but she couldn't stop the smile from touching her lips. "Miriam practically begged me to do it."

He crossed his arms over his chest. "Are you sure it wasn't the other way around?"

"I didn't even know you were the bachelor until Miriam told me."

"And that's when you said yes. You wanted an excuse to get close to me."

She playfully pushed his shoulder and tried not to notice the hard muscles beneath her fingers. "Shut up."

"So, it's true. You were happy I was the bachelor instead of Barros."

The jury was still out. Barros would have been easier in a lot of ways, but he definitely didn't give her butterflies like Grant did. She shook her head. "You're the worst."

"But you like me, admit it."

Oh, how she wanted to admit it. She really enjoyed the time she'd spent with Grant. He was so easy to be around, and he seemed so genuine. Em couldn't imagine him doing the things that her past boyfriends had done.

Of course, she hadn't imagined *them* betraying her either.

Now she could picture it perfectly.

Her stomach suddenly felt like it was full of lead, the butterflies long gone. She kept a brave smile on her face. "Keep dreaming, rookie."

"I haven't stopped since I first saw you."

Em's breath caught in her chest, and her smile fell. When he said sweet things like that, it made it much more difficult to pretend this was just a silly crush—that she wasn't really at risk of getting hurt. Flirting was much easier when they kept it light, just taking jabs at one another.

A blue card called on the other team's forward saved her from coming up with a reply to his heartbreakingly adorable comment. That meant the Storm would be up one player for the next two minutes.

Silence fell over her and Grant as they watched the game play in front of them. Or at least Em tried to watch the game. As much as she loved seeing her brother in action, it was difficult to focus on what was going on in front of her when Grant was sitting so close.

She was all too aware as he lifted the mug of beer to his lips. She couldn't help but notice the way his Adam's apple bobbed as he took a drink. Em lifted her own glass to her lips with trembling fingers and took a sip.

Why are you so nervous? As much as Grant teased, it still wasn't a real date. And she didn't want it to be. Or did she?

She took another sip of wine for good measure as she

watched Silas take a shot on goal. It was blocked by the other team's keeper.

"Did you really know it was me?" she asked, her eyes trained on the field.

"From the very first word. You made me speechless."

Miriam had jokingly said that during the game, but hearing it from Grant made her insides warm.

"But your not-so-subtle reference to my hometown helped."

She thought of McKensie and how Miriam had gone out of her way to stop the crazy chick from playing. "Not too stalker-y?"

"I thought it was sweet." He paused. "Just like your violin rendition."

Em covered her face with her hands. "It was pretty bad, wasn't it?"

Grant chuckled. "I think my ears bled a little."

She pushed him again. "What was I supposed to do? Be the third drum set? I panicked."

"I actually loved it. You weren't afraid to make a fool of yourself in front of all those people."

Her face burned. She could only hope none of the fans were recording the show on their phone. If anyone posted that, she was sure to be the butt of several online jokes. Thank goodness her students were too young to have cell phones, or they'd all see it for sure before Monday. "Well, I guess it goes to prove that people like the violin better than drums."

"I like *you*."

And there he went again, being all sweet and serious

and making Em break out into a sweat. Every time he said something like that, it lessened her resolve. She knew better than to fall for a smooth talking soccer player. If only there were some kind of test to see what kind of boyfriend Grant would be six months down the road.

She played with the stem of her glass. "You don't even know me."

"Isn't it enough that I want to? I know we don't know each other that well, but isn't that why you go on dates with people? To get to know them better?"

Em sighed. It felt like she was fighting an impossible battle. "Okay. Then let's say this is a real date. What kind of questions would you ask me over dinner?"

He sat up straighter, his eyes bright and eager. She didn't know if she should laugh or groan. "Well, I already know that Finn is your older brother, but you don't have any pictures of the rest of your family online."

Em blinked a few times. He was coming out swinging, and he didn't even know it. She bit her lip. "That's because Finn is the only family I have."

Grant reached out and grabbed her hand. His fingers were warm as they squeezed. "I'm so sorry, I didn't realize. How old were you when they died?"

"It's not like that." She pulled away her hand and shook her head. "Last time I checked, they were both very much alive, living out their lives in California."

His brows lowered. "I'm confused."

That made two of them. Em had made peace with the fact that her parents were complete pieces of crap years ago, but it always made questions like this uncomfortable for everyone.

She lifted her glass and swallowed the remaining contents of her glass. *Might as well get it over with. The sooner he knows, the sooner he can move on to someone normal.*

"Even though we lived with them until we graduated, they were never there." She shook her head. "Lucky for me, Finn has always been a good big brother. When I was little, he always helped me with my homework after school. When I got older, he helped me get my first job and taught me to drive. Finn is the one who went to the store and bought a pack of pads when I first got my period."

Her hand went to cover her mouth when she realized she'd said that last part. It was true, Finn had been the one who explained what was happening, despite being a young teenage boy at the time. But that wasn't exactly something you shared on a first date—or ever.

It had to be the wine that made her speak so freely. The possibility of her being this comfortable with Grant already was too terrifying to consider.

"I-I'm sorry. That was way too much information."

Grant gave her a small smile. "It wasn't the answer I was expecting to my question, but it means a lot that you were willing to share something so personal. Plus, it explains a lot."

"What does that mean?"

He ran a hand through his hair. "Only that I've seen how protective your brother is when it comes to you."

Em winced. "You heard about how he broke Parrera's nose, didn't you?"

And to think, they hadn't even dated. That poor guy had only expressed interest. How Damien got away with taking her on such a terrible date after that without any repercussions still baffled her. But it was also a relief. She hated when Finn got all macho man.

Grant nodded. "When Bastian first told me, I was shocked that Finn would act like that. But now it makes a little more sense. My big sister gets the same way." The corners of his mouth quirked up. "Though I don't think she's ever broken someone's nose over it."

Thankful for the shift in focus, Em smiled at Grant. "Maybe she's never had a good reason to."

He took a sip of his beer and leaned back in his chair. "Oh, I think she's had plenty of reasons. I've had my share of devastating breakups."

"You have?" Em couldn't imagine anyone breaking up with Grant.

"I went through a phase where I had really bad taste in girls."

She lifted a brow. "And how do you know you're not on a streak?"

Grant put both hands on the table and leaned forward. "Because she's already approved of you."

Em jerked back. "You told your sister about me?"

He shrugged. "Why wouldn't I? I figured you'd understand since you're so close to Finn."

She *was* close to her brother, but that didn't mean they talked about dating. Not anymore.

Speaking of her brother...Em had hardly given the game they were *supposed* to be watching a passing glance. She was too focused on the charming guy sitting with her.

The *soccer* player sitting with her.

Why was this so hard?

It felt like she was being torn in two every time she was with Grant.

Her heart told her to open up with Grant more, to see where things led. Even on the surface, he was better than the guys she'd dated. He was considerate—loved his family.

But her brain reminded her that opening up to him was a bad idea. Just because he seemed sweet now didn't mean he wouldn't pull a one-eighty like the other guys. What kind of ammunition had she just given him with her story about her parents? Plus, he lived in Kansas City. He wasn't going to stick around forever.

Fighting the panic rising in her chest, she stood up. "I've, uh, gotta go to the bathroom."

Confusion flashed over Grant's features.

Before he could say anything, she walked off—unsure of whether or not she was going to return.

13

GRANT

WELL, *this isn't going very well.*

Grant hadn't meant to scare Em off. He was only trying to find common ground after finding out what an awful childhood Em had. He'd mentioned that his sister had approved of Em instead of mentioning how supportive his parents were, but apparently that had been the wrong choice.

Why could he never seem to say the right thing to her once things got beyond the teasing? As long as they were joking and laughing, they were fine. But he'd finally had the chance to dig a little deeper, and he'd messed it up. Now he felt like a jerk and didn't know how he would turn things around.

When Em didn't return right away, Grant turned to the field. It was the first time he was truly watching the game since sitting down for their date. He could catch the replay online, but he only got one chance to make a good impression on Em.

Too bad he'd completely blown it.

The timer counted down through the final minute of the third quarter. When the buzzer sounded, the teams switched sides, putting Finn close to the VIP section. The keeper glanced over at Grant through lowered brows.

Grant was sure Finn was looking for his sister. He'd seen them leave the field together, and now she was gone. Grant's gaze went over his shoulder looking for Em. He'd done it about a million times in the ten minutes since she'd left. Every time he hoped to see her walking in his direction, and every time he was disappointed.

His gaze then went to the box seats next to the home bench. Miriam was still there, but she was alone. Frida had disappeared shortly after Em's hasty retreat and still hadn't returned.

At first, Grant had hoped they were doing that weird thing where girls went to the bathroom together. He knew Em probably needed to talk to her friend after their date went sideways. But now...

Now, he wondered if she was even still at the arena.

He'd only wanted to make a lasting impression on Em, not bring up all her childhood pain.

When the waitress walked by the table, Grant flagged her down and asked for the tab. The woman gave Grant a sympathetic smile and told him the drinks were on her.

Oh, great. Now the waitress feels sorry for me.

His attention went back to the game. The ball was in play on the other side of the field, and it was difficult to see the action. When Grant's eyes glanced over to Finn, he was surprised to see the keeper staring at him again. And it was less of a stare and more of a glare.

Grant shifted in his seat, his face growing hot under the continued scrutiny of Finn's narrowed eyes.

It wasn't like Grant had chosen to be the bachelor. Not only that, he didn't know Em would be one of the contestants. None of this was on purpose. He would just explain all of that to Finn when the game was over—and conveniently leave out the part about how he'd chosen Em once he realized it was her.

There was no sense in getting all worked up over things he couldn't change, especially now that it was painfully obvious she wasn't coming back to finish their date. In a way, Grant hadn't broken the no-dating-my-sister rule—he just hoped Finn would agree.

THE REST of the fourth quarter crawled by as Grant sat alone in the VIP section. The Storm scored two more goals and won the game with a final score of seven-to-three. When the players walked across the field toward the locker room, Grant pushed himself up on his crutches. He followed behind them feeling a little ridiculous in his suit and tie.

Since he'd been sitting the entire game, he took a spot against the wall as they all shuffled into the locker room. He leaned his back against the cool surface to take pressure off his leg and set the crutches to the side.

Coach immediately went into his recap of the game.

One by one, he called on players to give them a rundown of their strengths and weaknesses. "Grant."

His head jerked up, surprised that he was included. "Yes, Coach?"

"You just keep taking care of that ankle. I want you back out there playing as soon as possible, do you understand?"

Relief washed over him. It was good to know he was missed, even as a rookie. "You got it."

"Great." Coach continued to call on individual players to tell them what they needed to work on this week before the next game. They'd be traveling to Oregon and needed to be in peak performance. Playing in another team's arena always came with challenges, but dealing with such a drastic time change would make it even harder.

Coach clapped his hands together when he was done. "Get cleaned up, and get out there for the autograph session."

Grant grabbed his crutches, eager to get out there. Even though he didn't play, he would be on the field with a marker in hand. He didn't make it more than a couple steps before Finn approached him. The entire locker room was silent as the other players pretended not to watch out of the corners of their eyes.

Looked like he'd be explaining the non-date date sooner than he realized.

Grant cleared his throat, wishing they could have this talk without an audience. "Hey, Finn. Good game."

Flattery is always a good way to start, right?

"What's going on between you and my sister?"

His stomach dropped. *Or maybe not.* "What do you mean?"

Finn crossed his arms over his chest. Had his biceps always looked so big? "I saw you guys together after the halftime show."

Grant took a deep breath and tried to sound nonchalant. "Nothing's going on. Miriam asked me to be the bachelor tonight, and it looks like she somehow roped Em into it too."

"Emmeline."

"Right." Grant gave him a tight smile. "*Emmeline* was one of the contestants, and I chose her. I mean, I couldn't pick the girl with the skin-tight t-shirt. There are kids in the arena, and she'd have been hanging all over me. Totally inappropriate."

He hoped Finn didn't make the connection that Grant only knew she had a skin-tight shirt on *after* he'd already chosen Em.

Finn narrowed his eyes. "You're not dating my sister."

As if her walking out on me wasn't obvious enough.

Grant narrowed his eyes right back at Finn. This wasn't his fault...at least, not entirely. Miriam's meddling was at least fifty-percent responsible. "I'm not dating her. I'm participating in team events as required by my contract."

Finn's arms shifted to his sides, and Grant took an awkward step back on his crutches.

"It was just a silly halftime show," Silas said, rushing over. Bastian was right behind him. "It wasn't a real date.

She didn't even stay until the end, so she obviously wasn't into it."

Grant's chest tightened at the reminder, but Silas was right. It wasn't a real date, Em wasn't into him, at least, not after that disaster.

Silas put his hand on Finn's shoulder. "It's more like when you made Damien take Emmeline out and show her a bad time."

Finn shrugged off Silas's hand. "That was different, and you know it. I told Damien to take her out to protect her. That date was meant to turn her off athletes forever." Finn turned and narrowed his eyes at Grant. "I never asked *you* to do it."

Damien. He had to be the guy Em was talking about earlier. And now Grant knew why the date had been such a disaster. Grant's fists clenched at his sides at the thought. Em looked up to Finn. He was her big brother, and he was manipulating her, not protecting her. And what was Finn's issue with athletes? He was one, for crying out loud. What kind of captain thought so little of his teammates?

Grant took a deep breath through his nose, hoping to calm himself. He was still the rookie, and Finn was still his captain, misguided as his actions may be.

Grant lifted his chin. "I didn't know I needed your permission." Based on the looks on Silas and Bastian's faces, it was the wrong thing to say—though that wasn't entirely a surprise to him. He'd known he was dangerously close to doing something stupid.

Finn took a step toward Grant. "If you only knew

half the crap she's gone through. I won't let anyone hurt her."

Grant straightened his shoulders. "Anyone but you, you mean?"

Fire flashed in Finn's eyes. "I'm doing what's best for her."

Of course he'd think that. Grant was protective of his sister and had had a perfect childhood compared to what Em and Finn had been through as kids.

But they weren't kids anymore. Em was capable of making her own decisions. "Have you ever considered you might not be the right person to decide what's best for her?"

The only hint at what was to come were Finn's slightly narrowed eyes seconds before his fist connected with Grant's face. Pain exploded in Grant's eye and he fell back. His crutches fell away, and his hands circled madly for a few heart-stopping beats. Thankfully, he was close enough to the wall and was able to catch himself before stepping on his ankle and hurting it further. Not that it did anything for the pain that was now radiating through his entire head.

He took a step, using the wall to propel himself forward, and pulled his arm back. Two strong hands grabbed his shoulders and pushed him against the wall before he could swing.

There was a pinched expression on Bastian's face as he pinned him to the wall and hissed in his ear. "I told you not to mess around with Emmeline, and now you're provoking Finn? What is wrong with you?"

Grant looked over Bastian's shoulder at Finn. Silas was holding him back and spoke in hushed tones until Finn relaxed. Though he couldn't hear what was being said, Grant was sure Silas was trying to talk him down from coming for him again.

Let him come. I won't be caught off guard the second time.

"And people call me a hothead." All eyes turned to Vinny sitting on the bench, arms crossed and expression gleeful.

Finn made a growling sound and tried to maneuver around Silas—this time toward Vinny—but the forward held him back.

With Bastian, and everyone else in the locker room, distracted, Grant saw his opening. He would get Finn back, not only for himself, but for Em too. He pulled his shoulder free from Bastian's grip, but because of his injury, he wasn't able to get very far before Bastian pushed him back against the wall.

"You need to get a hold of yourself."

Grant fought for a few seconds before he relaxed against the wall. His teammate was right. He was letting his emotions get the best of him. But after having Em walk out, and then hearing that the one person she felt like she could trust wasn't as great as she thought, Grant was dangerously close to losing it.

He closed his eyes and took a couple deep breaths.

Bastian gripped his shoulder. "You need to listen to me."

Grant opened his eyes.

"Do not talk to Finn until he's had a chance to calm down. Do not go to the autograph session tonight. And for the love of all that is good and holy, do not talk to Emmeline again. Do you understand?"

Grant's gaze went to Finn.

Bastian squeezed his hand over the tight muscle between Grant's shoulder and neck. "Do you understand?"

Grant smacked Bastian's hand off of him and grabbed his crutches. "Yeah, I got it."

Not that he would actually listen to Finn or Bastian. It was one thing for Em to decide she didn't want to date, and quite another for Finn to say she was off-limits and sabotage her happiness with his fake date plan. She was a grown woman capable of making her own decisions.

Of course, she might not *want* to date him, he realized as he walked past the field on his way out of the arena.

But that was something he would need to hear from her mouth before he gave up on her.

14

EMMELINE

AFTER EVERYTHING that had happened at the game this past weekend, Em had been hoping for an easy week at school. Apparently, that was too much to hope for. She'd never been so relieved for Friday's dismissal bell. It was officially the weekend, and she kicked it off by crying in her car for fifteen minutes.

Riley, the student whose father recently died, was having a hard time after that morning's festivities. Not that Em could blame him.

Why did so many schools insist on having Donuts for Dads when there were so many broken families in the world? Sure, for many students—and their fathers—it was a great chance to hang out while stuffing their faces with sugary goodness.

But for others, like Riley, it only served as a reminder of what they didn't have.

Em knew that feeling all too well. Neither of her parents would have ever dreamed of showing up for a

Muffins with Mom or Donuts with Dad event. They'd never been on a single field trip, and couldn't be bothered to show up to any of Finn's soccer games back in high school.

Every time they didn't show up, it felt like a dagger to the heart. She always wondered what was wrong with her. Now that she was an adult, she knew the problem wasn't with her, but her parents. But her students were still too young to understand that.

She'd spent the week reminding her kids that any special person could be their guest for that morning's event, but either Riley hadn't realized that her gentle reminders were for him...or he didn't care.

She doubted it was the latter though based on the way he tried—and failed—to put on a brave face. She'd caught him with watery eyes on several occasions throughout the day. Em wanted to cry for him but had kept the tears at bay for his sake. She didn't want to draw more attention to him.

It wasn't fair. It wasn't Riley's fault that his dad died, just like it wasn't the other kids' fault that their parents had left, or didn't want to go. And yet, they were the ones who paid the price for it on these cutesy, themed breakfast days.

So she'd kept it together until the bell rang and even made it out to her car before the tears streamed down her cheeks. Her gentle crying had quickly become loud sobbing as all the emotions from her childhood came to her in a rush.

It was moments like this that she usually grabbed

takeout and showed up on Finn's doorstep. If she knocked on his door right now, he wouldn't turn her away—except for the pesky fact that he was on the other side of the country for an away game.

Em knew she could always go to her best friend with things like this too. Frida had always been there for Em growing up, but she was gone for the weekend at an art teacher conference, so she was also off the table.

Why did the two most important people to me have to disappear on the same weekend?

Em rested her forehead against her steering wheel and closed her eyes. There was only one other person who she'd opened up to about her awful parents, and she knew he was in town. Too bad she'd ghosted him in the middle of a date last week.

It would be completely unfair to expect Grant to talk to her after the way she'd treated him, she knew that. But she didn't know who else she could turn to.

It was possible she would show up to his house, and he would be gone doing something else. Or worse, he could have another girl over—that waitress had probably pounced the second Em had left the table last Saturday.

There was also the chance that Em would show up only to have Grant send her away. She wouldn't blame him.

But, said a tiny voice in her head, *what if he let me in?* Em had to hold on to that possibility. She took a deep breath and lifted her head from the steering wheel. After she composed herself, she pulled down the rearview mirror. There were giant black streaks running down both of her cheeks.

Yep. Grant might shut the door in my face.

But she had to try. Thankfully, she already knew where the team house was. She just needed to grab some food before she showed up on his doorstep. Luckily, she knew just where to go.

TWENTY MINUTES LATER, Em was standing outside a large, two-story bungalow in one of the nicer parts of town. A porch swing rocked gently in the breeze, and Em could see the edge of a lanai jutting out from the side of the house. The team's owners made sure the guys from out of town got the best Florida had to offer to entice them to stay. Em assumed the proximity to the best food trucks in town was a part of the strategy as well. She carried a bag in one hand while the other hovered just inches from the door.

Showing up unannounced had seemed like a good idea until she actually got there. Now, faced with the very real possibility of rejection, Em's stomach twisted in knots.

I shouldn't have come. If I leave right now, no one has to know I was even here...

She started to turn when the door opened with Grant on the other side. Her heart raced at the sight of him. He didn't have his crutches but was favoring his foot as he leaned against the doorjamb. Wearing a plain tee and athletic shorts, he looked very different from the last time she saw him.

A corner of his mouth lifted, but it wasn't quite a smile. "I hope you don't mind that I didn't wait for you to knock. It's not exactly easy getting up and down these days."

Em wanted to crawl under a rock. She'd been standing in front of the door for longer than she'd realized while she dithered—and he'd known she was there the entire time.

She opened her mouth to explain but noticed a shadow of a bruise under one of his eyes. She lifted her hand to his cheek. "What happened?"

He turned his face causing her fingers to fall. "Nothing."

It didn't look like nothing. *What kind of trouble are you getting into, Grant?* Instead of pushing, she asked, "What are you up to?"

Grant stared at her, his expression still unreadable. "Just hanging out. Why?"

Em lifted the bag in her hand. "I thought you might be hungry."

Grant looked at her for a long time. His eyes went to the bag in her hands. "What is it?"

His question gave her hope.

She smiled. "Tacos from my favorite food truck."

Em's entire body sagged in relief when he stepped to the side and waved one of his hands for her to come in.

Once inside, she went straight to the kitchen. It had been a while since she'd been to the team house, and she'd forgotten how sterile the place was. It was nicely decorated, like a hotel, but it had no personality.

He leaned against the kitchen counter and watched Em as she pulled out two Styrofoam trays covered in aluminum foil. Each one contained five authentic Mexican tacos with chicken, diced onions, and cilantro—her favorite thing from the taco truck. She hoped Grant would like it too.

"What are you doing here, Em?"

Her hands stilled on the small containers of salsa and loose lime slices in the bottom of the bag. "I brought you dinner. Tacos from the place I mentioned during *The Dating Game*."

"Yeah, I assumed. I'm asking *why* you're here." He shook his head. "You left me high and dry on our date, I haven't heard from you all week, and then you show up on my doorstep with food."

"Not just any food. *Tacos*."

He lifted his brows.

He was expecting an answer. She bit her bottom lip as she struggled to come up with one. *Why am I here?*

Em hadn't wanted to admit it earlier, but now she was at Grant's house—and he was looking at her with his intense blue eyes—she had to face the reality.

She was here because, at some point between flirting with Grant at City Bar and showing up on his doorstep, he'd become someone she wanted to spend time with. The no-dating-players rule existed to protect her heart, but it was too late. As much as she'd tried to fight against it, she cared for Grant.

But she was scared. Scared of being rejected—of being hurt again. And that fear had caused her to treat Grant unfairly.

She squeezed her eyes shut. "I...I'm pretty sure I like you. I know I haven't been very good at showing you that. I ditched you on Saturday, which was pretty awful. If you want me to leave, I'd understand."

"Hey now. Let's not get too hasty." Grant said with a hint of humor in his voice. "I don't want you to go. I'm just confused."

That makes two of us.

She kept her eyes shut and nodded. "Me too."

Grant was silent for a long time. Em wasn't sure what happened next. Were they going to have an awkward talk about defining their relationship? Was he going to tell her he'd changed his mind, but they could still be friends?

The knots in her stomach from earlier returned with a vengeance. They twisted tightly and just when Em didn't think she could stand it anymore, she heard Grant push off the wall. Her breath caught when he walked over to where she still stood next to the food. She opened her eyes and looked up at him.

He had a warm smile on his face. "I was going to eat a bowl of cereal for dinner. Tacos sound much better."

That was not the reaction she was expecting, but it was exactly what she needed after the difficult day she'd had. How did Grant know that she wasn't ready to work out the details just yet?

Em let out a relieved breath and shook her head. "You're such a helpless bachelor."

"Not anymore." He jerked his chin at the food. "A pretty girl who likes me brought me food. I'd say I'm living the dream."

"You're the worst."

His brows lowered. "You say that, but you just admitted your gigantic crush on me. I'd have to question if you even know what that word means."

Em's face felt like it was on fire, but she giggled and lifted one of the lime slices and squirted it over her tacos. If he wanted to keep things light, then so could she. "I don't remember using the words 'gigantic crush.' Must be your male ego inflating things."

"Probably." He popped a stray piece of chicken into his mouth and leaned against the counter.

"So what *were* you planning on doing before that pretty girl showed up at your doorstep? Other than eating cereal."

He shrugged as he followed her lead and grabbed a lime of his own. "I was going to watch the game and feel sorry for myself."

"Ooh. Sounds exciting."

He lowered his voice to whisper. "Very."

Em's entire body shivered. "We can still do that, you know. The game starts in fifteen minutes. Just enough time to eat and get comfortable before kickoff."

"Sounds good." Grant grabbed his tray and walked out to the living room. In it was a sofa with a small coffee table. On the opposite wall there was a TV on top of a simple stand. The only piece of art on the walls was a generic ocean scene.

Just another empty, boring room.

Em had never stopped to think about how strange it must feel living in a house that wasn't really yours—knowing you wouldn't be there longer than the season. There was no reason to make it feel homey, and yet it made her sad to think that this was where Grant spent his days.

They both sat down on the sofa and put their trays on the table in a choreographed way like they'd been doing this together for years. Tacos on the couch while they watched a game. Is this what Friday and Saturday nights would look like if they were dating?

No, because he'd be playing again soon. But maybe it would be the latest episode of their favorite show when the season was over. She pushed the thought down, still unsure of what to make of the feelings building between them.

Grant sat on the end of the couch and lifted one of the tacos. "Here's the moment of truth." He leaned forward and took a bite. His eyes closed when he started chewing, and Em swore she heard a moan from the back of his throat.

Is he for real?

"Wow." He opened his eyes and looked at Em. "These are really *yummy.*"

That was the word Frida had used to describe Grant in the school cafeteria. Even though Em had just admitted that she liked him, she was still embarrassed that he'd picked up on Frida's not-so-subtle comments from that day. A blush crept up her throat, and she turned and took a bite of her taco in an attempt to hide it.

"Aw, don't be embarrassed," he teased. "You can't help it if you have good taste."

Em swallowed her bite. "You really are in love with yourself, aren't you?"

He shook his head. "Not really. I just like the way you look when I say things like that."

Like a hormonal teenager who just discovered boys for the first time? Because that was certainly how she felt whenever he acted like this. Her cheeks always felt hot with a blush, she got oddly giggly, and her stomach did weird things.

"What about all your workout videos on Instagram? You seem to love posting hot and sweaty selfies." She lifted her brows.

"Hot and sweaty? Is that the persona I'm putting off?" He laughed and turned in his seat so that he faced her head-on. "I just do that to help build my online personality. Silas is always going on about building your brand and trying to attract the attention of different companies to increase your revenue."

"Seriously?"

"If it was up to me, I wouldn't do all that." He stopped and smiled to himself. "Actually, that's a lie."

Em knew it sounded way too good to be true.

"I would keep doing them because of the way it feels to see you like each post. It gives me a thrill to know you're watching me so closely."

"I don't..." Her words trailed off when she realized

she'd be lying if she said she didn't watch his profile. And she loved that he did the same. She looked up at him with wide eyes.

Grant leaned forward and lifted his hands to her face. "It's okay. I like you, Em. I've never made that a secret. You're the one who wanted to pretend there wasn't anything going on between us."

He was right. She'd always been the one to push him away due to her stupid no-dating athletes rule. Grant was amazing, and he liked her. Why was she fighting it?

With their dinner forgotten and getting cold on the table, she wet her lips and closed the distance between them.

15

GRANT

EM'S LIPS were soft and hesitant as they pressed against Grant's.

He was so shocked that he didn't move at first. He'd wanted this since the first time he'd spotted her in the arena, and now that Em was here, in his house, *kissing him,* he wasn't doing anything.

What is wrong with you?

She pulled back, her eyes wide. "I'm sorry, I thought..."

She thought that he wasn't kissing her because he didn't want her? Nothing could be further from the truth.

True, Grant needed to stay focused on his goals, and dating someone would make it difficult to stay on track. Not only that, Finn had told him to stay away from her. The other teammates on the Storm had warned him that getting mixed up with Em was a bad idea. Even Em had repeatedly said that she didn't date soccer players.

None of that had been enough to deter him.

Grant wanted Em more than he could stand.

His eyes went to her lips that were now turned down into a frown. If he didn't do something he would lose his chance. He might not get another one.

His heart hammered in his chest as he put his hands on either side of her face. Her skin was soft beneath his fingertips. He closed his eyes and brought his lips down on hers. The kiss was gentle at first, but when she sighed into his mouth, his lips became more demanding.

Now *this* was a kiss.

His hands slid to the back of her head, and he ran his fingers through her hair. Her arms wrapped around his shoulders, and her fingers curled into the muscles of his back. It was all the encouragement he needed to slide a hand down her back to pull her closer. She'd been so close yet so far for weeks; he needed her pressed as tightly to him as possible. Her fingers gripped his shirt.

This moment was the culmination of weeks of flirting and dancing around each other, and now they were finally coming together. Grant lost all sense of himself. There was only Em. Only her soft lips, her silky hair, the smell of her shampoo invading his senses. He never wanted to stop kissing her, and he was afraid if he didn't pull away soon, he never would.

He leaned away, his breaths coming in sharp, jagged bursts. When he opened his eyes, he could see Em's chest rising and falling just as quickly. Her lips were swollen, and she had a dazed look in her eyes.

She'd never looked more beautiful.

He took a shaky breath. "Wow."

She wet her lips and nodded. "Uh-huh."

"Tell me why we didn't do that sooner?"

She closed her eyes. "Because I don't date athletes."

Grant was getting really tired of that line. She said it all the time without giving any good reason behind it. They'd just kissed, and she was still reciting it. "But why?"

She bit her bottom lip and shook her head. "I've always found them to care too much about themselves to have room for anyone else."

That's why she mentioned my "workout" videos. She thinks I'm self-absorbed.

"I'm not like that. I only post so much about myself to get visibility. Once the camera is gone, I don't care. I just told you that."

Em put a hand to his chest, and he calmed. "I know. But it's more than that. I've been hurt so many times."

Grant already knew about the disaster with Damien. He also knew it was an awful set up coordinated by her *loving* brother. Other than that, he couldn't imagine anyone wanting to hurt her. He pushed down the anger that came with that thought and reached out to grab one of her hands. "What happened?"

She looked up at him with wide eyes. "Do you really want to know?"

"Only if you want to tell me."

"The only other person who knows everything is Frida. It's not something I talk about, but for some reason, I trust you." She lifted a shoulder. "Maybe hearing these stories will make you understand why I'm so hesitant to trust another athlete again."

He squeezed her hand hoping it would encourage her.

She took a deep breath. "I didn't date a lot in high school. I mean, I might go to a dance with a guy friend, but it was never serious."

Grant was sure every single one of those guy friends wanted something more, but he kept his mouth shut, knowing she needed to say it all without interruption.

"But my junior year, I started hanging out with this guy named Travis. He played varsity soccer with Finn. He seemed like a really cool guy. We had a lot of fun together, but he always wanted to take things a little further than I was comfortable. He had a lot more experience than I did since he was my first real boyfriend."

A sinking feeling of dread settled in Grant's stomach. He had a feeling he knew where this was going. He wanted her to stop, knowing she was about to relive something that was very painful for her, but he wanted her to know she could trust him.

"He told me that he loved me and that he was always going to be there for me. I thought I loved him too, but I see now I was just desperate for anyone other than my brother to find me worthy." She looked down, tears shining in her eyes. "But silly me couldn't tell the difference. So when he wanted us to 'go all the way' one night, I let him." She closed her eyes. "The next day he showed up to school with another girl. He didn't even bother breaking up with me properly."

"Em."

She shook her head. "It's okay. It's not like I'm the first girl who's fallen for that trick, right?"

Her voice was light and airy, but Grant saw the glistening of unshed tears in her eyes. She lifted her shoulder. "Anyway, when Finn saw him with his tongue shoved down the other girl's throat, he beat the crap out of him—and that was without him knowing all the details."

Grant didn't want to think what would have happened to that poor sucker if Finn *had* known.

"So, I swore off guys for the next year. But then I met Mark in college. He was another soccer player and so sweet. I told him right off the bat that I wanted to take things slow, and he agreed. We dated for two years. I thought we were going to get married. But then he slowly drifted away. He became obsessed with working out and watching clips of himself playing. He wanted to play for the EPL and didn't have time for me. He dumped me on Valentine's Day. Thankfully, Finn was in a different state that time."

What a jerk.

"You'd think I'd learned my lesson, right? Soccer players were bad news. But then Finn started playing for the Storm, and I was hanging out with players after the games. I got a little flirty with some of them. Even after Finn broke Parrera's nose for hitting on me, I didn't want to listen. When Damien asked me out, I jumped at the chance."

Grant had to bite the inside of his cheek to stop himself from saying that Finn had told Damien to do it.

"I don't know if I even liked him. Maybe I went out with him just to spite Finn. Either way, it was a huge mistake."

"How so?" Grant leaned forward, eager to hear what happened on the date Finn had secretly ordered.

"He didn't hurt me like the others. It was more comically bad than anything else." She laughed to herself. "He wouldn't stop talking about himself. When my car battery died, he left me stranded at the restaurant with the bill. Thankfully, Finn was able to rescue me. He's the only one I can always count on to be there."

Grant fought to keep his expression neutral, but just beneath the surface his blood was boiling. Em trusted her brother even though he was just as bad as the other guys, not that Grant could tell her that. It would crush her to know that Finn had been keeping secrets of his own and controlling her life.

"Which brings me to you," Em said, pulling him from his quiet rage. "I've been struggling with what to think about you, Grant. I've been afraid to admit that I like you because I don't want to get hurt again."

Of course, she was hesitant to open herself up to him. All she'd known were jerks, but she had to see that he was different. "I would never hurt you like that."

"You say that now, but what happens when you go back to Kansas City or another team recruits you or the EPL expresses interest? You're a rookie with your entire career ahead of you." She looked down at her hands folded in her lap.

Grant leaned back against the futon and covered his face with his hands. He let out a long breath. She was right. He didn't want to admit it because he really liked her and would never hurt her intentionally, but there was so much uncertainty in his future.

He was still injured and didn't know when he would be able to play soccer again. If he didn't get enough time with the team, he wasn't sure if the Storm would sign him on for another season. Not only that, when the season was over, he planned to go home to Kansas City.

He might not be like Travis, Mark, or even Damien—but that didn't mean he wouldn't break her heart. He never wanted to do that to her. She didn't deserve it. He needed to end things before they went any further.

"You're right."

Her head snapped up. "What?"

Apparently, it wasn't the answer she was hoping for. *Trust me, I don't like it either.* He shook his head. "I'm going back to Kansas City in the spring when the season is over. I don't know if I'll be back. A long-distance relationship wouldn't be fair to either of us."

Her eyes glistened again, and Grant felt like a real jerk knowing he was the one who put those tears there this time. *Now I'm just another guy in the long list of people who hurt you.*

Em opened her mouth like she was going to say something, and Grant knew he didn't have the resolve to fight against her if she suggested they try anyway. If she showed even a hint of wanting to be with him, in a heartbeat he would pull her against him, kiss her, and beg her not to go.

But then she pressed her lips together and shook her head. "Goodbye, Grant."

Then she got up and walked out the front door without another word or even a glance back.

16

EMMELINE

FOR THE SECOND time that day, Em was crying in her car. And the worst part? There wasn't anyone left that she could talk to about it. Finn was in the middle of playing a soccer game she hadn't watched a minute of because she was too busy making out with Grant and then getting her heart broken.

What was it about her that said, "please break my heart into a million pieces?"

When she'd said that thing about him having so many options, she didn't think he was going to agree—not based on the way he'd pursued her the last few weeks.

Don't act surprised. Your rule exists for a reason.

She'd thought he was different. She'd thought he'd fight for her—especially when she'd shared things with him that she hadn't shared with anyone else.

Well, anyone other than Frida. Em was newly frustrated. Why did her best friend's art teacher conference have to be the same weekend as her brother's away game? The timing couldn't have been worse.

Em wiped furiously at her cheeks, again, and got out of her car. Her current plan consisted of trying to catch the last half of the game. It wasn't the most exciting thing in the world, but she hoped seeing her brother—even from 2,500 miles away—would make her feel better.

Her feet dragged as she walked up the flight of stairs to her second-story apartment. With a sigh, she threw her keys on the small table by her front door and went to her kitchen to look for something to eat.

Her kitchen was smaller than the one at the team house, but at least it had more personality. There were pictures on the refrigerator, and her copy of *Pioneer Woman Cooks* was still open to the recipe for chicken pot pie that she'd made two nights ago. Too bad there wasn't any left. She could really use the comfort food instead of whatever frozen meal awaited her.

She tried not to think about the tacos she left behind as the aroma of "chicken fettuccine" filled the air. Or the way Grant had literally moaned when he took his first bite.

I hope he chokes on them.

After she finished nuking her meal into oblivion, she grabbed the small tray of food and went out to her living room. She pulled up the game and leaned back against her couch. She'd missed the first half, but at least she'd get to watch some of the game.

The Storm was down two goals as they started the third quarter. Em knew that had to be driving her brother crazy. Even though there were five other players on the field, he saw every ball that got past him as a way he let the team down.

One of the forwards from Oregon took a shot on goal. When Finn blocked it, Em jumped up in her seat. It was a great save. The camera lingered on where Finn pumped his fist in victory just before he barked out orders to other players.

As Em watched the game and finished her dinner, she realized that this was exactly what she needed. Even though she was alone in her apartment, there was some normalcy to watching her brother and the rest of the guys play. Silas made two back-to-back goals making it a tie game at the end of the third quarter.

The two teams were evenly matched, making it an exciting game to watch. So exciting, in fact, that she only thought about Grant twice in that time and only peeked at his Instagram once. Even though they weren't officially dating, it stung like a breakup. It would take time for her to get completely over him. She knew that she couldn't just turn on a soccer game and pretend like none of that night, or the weeks leading up to it, had ever happened.

The Storm called a time out at the start of the fourth quarter. While the ball was out of play, the camera went to different people in the crowd. Kids dressed in Oregon colors who waved. Couples who gave each other chaste kisses when they realized they were on the giant screen in the arena. Then a lone fan sitting by herself in a Storm jersey that looked awfully familiar.

Wait. Was that...*Frida?*

It couldn't be. She was at a teacher's convention that weekend. In Alabama. Or at least that's what Frida had told her before she left. Em leaned forward to get a better look at the girl on the screen. She was looking down at the field, blissfully unaware that the camera was on her.

It *was* Frida—and she was wearing the limited-edition jersey that Em had spent a fortune on.

Em turned off the TV and started pacing back and forth in her living room. Her best friend had flown all the way to Oregon to watch a Storm game without her. What was worse, she had lied about it.

Em tried to think of the reasons Frida would go. As far as she knew, Frida wasn't even that big of an MASL fan. She hadn't started going to games until recently.

She sat back down and pulled out her phone. Her hands shook as she texted Frida and asked her how the conference was.

Her response came just a moment later.

> It's okay. Boring.

Em squeezed her hands into small fists. Was everyone she cared about going to disappoint her tonight?

First it was Grant with their pseudo-breakup. Then, Frida had lied about where she was. The only person who hadn't betrayed her was Finn.

Finn.

All the air swooshed from Em's lungs as the realization hit her. Frida was there to see Finn play. She was sure of it. And they'd been keeping it a secret. Em couldn't believe they'd been lying to her. She wondered what else she didn't know.

Her fingers flew across the screen.

> How long have you two been dating?

This time Frida took much longer to respond. Em's finger tapped impatiently on her thigh as she waited for an answer. Eventually it came.

> How did you know?

So, it was true. Seeing the words hit hard even though she was sure her suspicions were right.

> How long?

Frida's response came faster this time.

> Two months. I wanted to tell you, but Finn thought we should wait.

Two months? That was a long time to keep a secret, and Em only knew her best friend and brother were dating because of an Oregon cameraman with a sense of humor.

She wanted to cry, but she'd already shed enough tears that day. Em powered down her phone, turned the TV off, and went to bed—though it was several hours before sleep finally overpowered her.

17

GRANT

GRANT WALKED INTO BIG RESULTS, alone.

He could now walk without his crutches or a limp, but he still had another week until his doctor and the Storm's athletic trainer would let him do regular workouts with the rest of the team.

Not that he wanted to see the rest of the team after what had happened.

Since the scene in the locker room, Grant hadn't had more than a passing "hello" with his roommates. Grant tried to leave the team house just before his roommates got back from Big Results. That way he wouldn't see them at home. And by the time he got to the gym, they'd all cleared out. It had been working out perfectly.

Cool air hit him as he entered the large building. He might not have been allowed to workout as hard as he wanted to, but he could still focus on his core and upper body—as well as run through the exercises he'd been given to strengthen his ankle and promote faster healing.

Grant didn't put any unnecessary strain on his foot other than when he'd blocked the ball for Em. He followed doctor's orders to a tee in hopes of getting back to the game sooner, but now he wondered if that was what he really wanted. Of course he wanted to play. Soccer was his life. But everything that happened with Finn tainted the game for him.

Grant lifted some weights from the rack and started doing bicep curls in front of the mirrored wall. He was so consumed with his thoughts that he didn't notice Bastian until he'd finished his first rep.

The defender crossed his arms over his chest. "You're a hard guy to get a hold of."

Grant didn't bother holding back his groan. "What are you doing here?"

Bastian took a long drink from his water bottle. "I thought I'd spend some time working on my arms."

Grant highly doubted that. He set the weights back on the rack. "Why are you really here?"

Bastian released a long sigh. He jerked his head toward the front of the gym. There was a small in-house café with several small tables in front of it. "Wanna sit for a minute? Get a smoothie?"

He'd come to workout and just walked through the door. Sitting and having a drink with Bastian was the last thing he wanted to do. He narrowed his eyes. "Not really."

Bastian surprised him by laughing. "I'm not here to fight with you, Grant. I just want to talk."

Grant lifted his hands. "What is there to talk about?"

Bastian looked down at Grant's feet. "Your ankle?"

"Still sprained."

"Finn?"

"Still a jerk."

"Look." Bastian shook his head. "I'm not the bad guy here."

Grant took a step toward him. "Aren't you though? Maybe not to me, but you and everyone else on the team want to all pretend like what Finn is doing to Em is okay. I question it and end up on the receiving end of his right-hook."

"I'm sorry, man."

Grant's blood was boiling. He didn't want Bastian's apology. He wanted everyone to stop letting Finn manipulate Em. "Maybe you guys don't see it because you've been playing together for so long, but this whole thing is messed up."

"I—"

"And based on what you told me that first night at City Bar, it's not the first time Finn has let his temper get the best of him. No one is going to stand up to him, so why don't you just say what you came here to say."

Bastian rubbed a hand over his face. "Fine. I came here to find out if you're still talking to Em. She's been ignoring Finn, and he thinks it's because you guys are dating."

Finn again. Grant's answering laugh was cruel. "If that's the case, then why doesn't *he* ask me about it?"

"Because we won't let him. Vinny has been running interference so that he doesn't show up to your house."

Grant couldn't believe the same guy who had delighted in Grant and Finn's fight was now trying to prevent another from happening. "Really?" he asked.

"No one wants this kind of conflict on the team. It shows up on the field."

"I'm not even on the field," he yelled, drawing the attention of some people using the machines. Soon, he'd be stealing Vinny's nickname for his explosive attitude.

Grant smiled and lifted his hand in a small, apologetic wave. He and Bastian walked away from the equipment, so they were no longer in full sight of everyone.

After a beat of silence, Bastian spoke. "I know it's gotta be tough having an injury your first year, but you'll be out there playing again in another week or two. When that happens, we need to be united so that we can win. Not fighting over some girl."

"Some girl? Em is not just some girl. She's amazing."

Bastian's eyes went wide. "And you're gonna stick to the 'not dating' story?"

Grant shook his head. "We're not."

Though I wish we were.

"Then why isn't Em talking to her brother?"

"Sounds like a question her brother needs to ask her. I haven't seen her since—" He stopped short not wanting to tell Bastian about the night they kissed. That was a special moment between just the two of them, even if it ended in heartbreak for them both.

"Since?"

Grant shook his head. "Since the night she walked out on me."

There. That wasn't technically a lie. She'd walked out twice now. The first time had been in front of the entire team, and Bastian smiled sympathetically, not questioning it further.

"Can I workout now? Or is there any other high school drama that needs to be addressed?"

Bastian's face fell. "No, that was it."

Grant instantly felt bad for snapping at him. As Bastian had said earlier, *he* wasn't the bad guy. Finn was the one ruining everyone's lives with his overprotectiveness of Em. Grant was so tired of the senselessness of it all.

So much so, that he might have ended things with Em if they weren't already over.

Liar.

"Good. Because I've gotta get back to my workout."

"Right." Bastian nodded. "We're all looking forward to you coming back."

Grant didn't say anything before he turned and walked back to the weight room where he spent the next hour trying—and failing—not to think about Em.

LATER THAT DAY, after Grant had gotten home and showered, he spent some time looking at master's programs.

His injury had given him a lot to think about. He would be able to play again soon, just as Bastian had said, but Grant had to start thinking seriously about what his exit strategy was. He wouldn't be able to play forever—eventually he'd get too old, too slow. Or even worse, there was always the possibility of another injury, one that put him out permanently.

Grant needed to know that he'd be able to get a nine-to-five when that happened.

Since he wasn't ready to put on a suit and tie just yet, he figured furthering his education in the meantime was a good place to put his energy. Now that Em was out of the picture, he could focus on soccer, build his online brand, and go to school.

With so much on his plate, he wouldn't have time to think about how he'd missed out on something special with Em.

As he researched different schools, he came across USF. Only an hour from Waterfront, the university boasted several flexible schedules to get your master's. He could do a combination of summer classes and online classes that fit around soccer season.

If he went to school there, he could stay in Florida.

Why are you doing this to yourself?

It was a stupid thing to do, but applying didn't mean that he was committed to going there. And going there didn't mean that he had to stay in Waterfront. He could always move to Tampa. But even if he *did* stay in town, that didn't mean he was trying to find a way to make things happen with Em.

Or was he?

The pain of calling things off with her was too fresh

in his mind for him to think clearly. He knew that. Which was why after he finished his expedited application for the school, he applied for three more—all in the Midwest, all close to home.

Though Kansas City was feeling less and less like home the more time he spent in Florida.

18

EMMELINE

"YOU CAN'T IGNORE ME FOREVER," Frida said, storming into Em's empty classroom after school on Wednesday.

After using two personal days earlier in the week, Em was back at school—and completely behind. The sub that had filled in for her hadn't used any of the lesson plans she'd left. Now she was playing catch up and really didn't have the energy to deal with Frida. She knew she should have taken everything home to avoid this exact moment. Or maybe she subconsciously knew that they needed to talk, and that was why she had stayed.

"I wasn't ignoring you." Em's eyes were trained on a stack of papers she needed to grade.

"Really?" Frida pulled one of the student's chairs over to Em's desk and sat down. "Because I've called and texted with no response. I even showed up at your apartment and knocked on the door for thirty minutes with no answer before finally leaving."

Those had been some of the longest minutes of Em's life. The entire time she'd been worried that one of her neighbors would call the cops. Thankfully, they hadn't, and Frida had eventually left.

She shrugged. "I must not have been home."

"Emmeline O'Brien, your car was in the parking lot."

"Then I must have been taking a nap." She played with the cap of her red pen.

Frida narrowed her eyes. "Since when do you take naps?"

Em smacked her hands on her desk. "What do you want, Frida?"

Frida's chin trembled. "You're my best friend. I want you to stop ignoring me. I want you to talk to me." She leaned forward. "You're upset about me and Finn. We kept it a secret from you, and we shouldn't have. I know that. But I can't change that now. All I can do is try to work things out with you."

It was more than keeping it a secret though. They were the two people in her life that she thought she could trust, and they lied to her. Em fought back the tears that filled her eyes. They were not going to fall right now. She'd cried enough the last few days. She would not shed another tear.

Frida got up and walked around the desk. She bent over and wrapped her arms around Em. "I should have told you."

Never mind. Her best friend's words put her over the edge. Tears streamed down her cheeks. "Why didn't you tell me? I would have been happy for you guys."

Frida stood back up, and she smoothed out her skirt even though there were no wrinkles. "I wanted to, but I know you have your no-dating-athletes rule."

That stupid rule was more trouble than anything else. She shook her head. "That's my rule, not yours."

"I know, but you're convinced every athlete is evil. I wasn't sure what you'd say."

Not every athlete was bad, just the ones she fell for. Besides, Finn was her brother.

"I would have given you my blessing."

Frida lifted her brows. "And now?"

Nothing had changed. Em still loved Frida and Finn more than anyone else. She wanted them to be happy. And she didn't get to say whether or not they dated. At this point, she had to decide whether or not she would be happy for them. "I think it's great."

"Really?"

Em nodded.

"Oh, good." Frida lit up. "Because I really like him. He's so funny and sweet and he looks really good out there on the field with his muscles straining."

"I might be okay with you two dating, but he's still my brother. I don't want to hear how good he looks or anything about his muscles straining." Em lifted the corners of her mouth into a smile.

Frida laughed. "Fine. No muscles. But he's one of the good ones. He makes me happy." She paused. "It's why I kept bidding on that stupid jersey. I wanted it so bad."

Em's eyes went wide. "*You're* the one who I got into that bidding war with?"

Frida's cheeks turned a deep red. "It was right after that game that we started dating. I thought it would have been cool to have it. I had no idea you were willing to go so high."

"Then it's yours."

Frida sat up. "Really?"

Em nodded. "I have plenty. And it means a lot to you."

"Thank you."

"You're welcome. I'm glad you guys are happy." And she was. But knowing how perfect Frida and Finn were for each other only made her failed relationship with Grant more painful. With time, it would get easier. It always did. But for now, everything was just a little too overwhelming.

"And things are okay between us?"

"Yeah." Em smiled at her. "Just don't lie to me anymore. You're my best friend."

"Deal," Frida said.

"Good." Em looked down at the stack of papers in front of her. "But now that we're not fighting anymore, I really need to finish grading these papers."

Frida grabbed a red pen from the jar on Em's desk.

"What are you doing?"

Frida rolled her eyes. "Helping you, duh. What are friends for?"

Em smiled as she divided the papers into two piles. She was so thankful for her friendship with Frida. It would be an adjustment to see her and Finn together, but Em would get used to it in time.

They had only been grading papers for a few minutes when Frida set her pen down. "Have you talked to Grant at all since *The Dating Game*?"

The Dating Game. That night felt like it was an eternity ago with everything else that had happened since—and Frida didn't know about any of it. The last thing Frida knew about was Em walking out on Grant. Her best friend had met her in the bathroom and made no secret of the fact that she thought Em should go back in there and see where things went.

Thankfully, Frida had also been supportive when Em said she needed to get out of there.

Em nodded. "Yeah."

"Really?" Frida sat up in her seat.

"I, uh, went to his house when you were in Oregon."

Frida's mouth fell open. "You what?"

She bit her bottom lip. "I had a bad day at work, and you were gone. I realized he'd become someone I wanted to spend time with as much as I tried to fight it. I brought him tacos."

"That's adorable. So, what happened?"

Em folded her arms on her desk and put her head down. "I kissed him." The words came out as a mumble as she spoke into the crook of her arm.

"You kissed him?"

Em nodded, her head still on her desk.

"Does that mean…?"

Em lifted her head, her heart still heavy from that night. "No. He said that things wouldn't work out between us."

"He said those exact words?"

"Not exactly, but that was the gist."

"Oh, Em. I'm so sorry."

She shrugged, her eyes trained on the jar of pencils on her desk. "I'm sure it's for the best."

Not that it felt like it was for the best right now. Right now it hurt—bad.

There was a long pause and Em had gone back to grading when Frida spoke again.

"Do you think you'll go to the rest of the Storm games since you'll have to see him?"

What did it say about Em that she hadn't even thought about that?

On one hand, she wanted to go out and support Finn. Even though she hadn't spoken to him in days, he was still her brother. And now that he was dating Frida, Em would need to make sure Finn didn't get distracted the same way Silas did whenever he ran past Miriam.

On the other hand, Em also wasn't sure how she would react once she saw Grant out there. It would be hard to cheer on the guy who broke her heart. Or stop thinking about the way his lips felt when they pressed against hers.

Her heart hammered in her chest at the memory. As much as she tried to stop thinking about what had happened, her brain thought it belonged on the highlight reel and replayed it every chance it got. Em couldn't figure out why she couldn't just forget about it.

Because it was the best kiss of my life.

"I don't know," she said, finally answering Frida's

question. "I think it's going to depend on my mood when Saturday rolls around. And even if I go, I'll probably hide in the stands instead of sitting in my box."

Frida's shoulders slumped.

"But you can still use Finn's tickets. I'm sure Miriam would enjoy the company." *And getting her girlfriends only cheering section...*

She shook her head softly. "I couldn't."

"You can." Em reached out to grab her hand. "Really, I'll be fine."

"Em."

"Who knows," she said, trying to keep her tone light. "I may end up sitting down next to the field after all."

It was highly unlikely, but possible.

"I'm sure Finn would like that."

Finn.

Now that the two friends had tackled their friendship and what had happened with Grant, it was the only tough conversation left to have.

She sighed loudly.

"He's really upset. He's been asking me every day if I've talked to you. And every time I say no, he looks a little more broken."

Em's chest tightened. She hated that she'd hurt her brother. While she had every right to be upset, she found her irritation lessening every day. Now that she'd made up with Frida, it was practically nonexistent.

"I'll talk to him tonight," she said, her attention going back to the paper she'd been trying to grade for the last five minutes.

Frida let out a dramatic sigh. "I planned to spend some one-on-one time with him when I was done here."

When Em's head snapped up, Frida burst into loud laughter. "Oh my goodness. It's going to be so fun messing with you."

Em shook her head, but she was happy to see that even though Frida was dating her brother, that some things wouldn't change.

19

GRANT

GRANT'S STOMACH twisted in knots as he got dressed in his game day kit with the rest of the team.

It had been hard watching the rest of the players practice without him for the last few weeks—harder to watch them play while he sat on the sidelines. Even though his ankle had fully recovered, everything felt a little off.

Bastian was too cheerful. Finn was too distant. And it seemed like everyone else was watching out of the corner of their eyes to see what would happen now that Grant was back.

He sat on the bench to tie his shoe and tried to ignore the simmering tension and get his head ready for the game when Cardosa plopped down beside him.

"How's the ankle feeling?" he asked, jerking his head down at Grant's foot.

People had been asking him that all week, and it was

starting to get on his nerves. If he wasn't ready to play, he wouldn't be kitted out, would he?

"Good. As long as I don't push it too hard tonight, I think it'll be fine."

Cardosa slapped his back. "We're all glad you're back."

"Are you?"

Cardosa's brows lowered. "Of course we are."

He lifted his brows. "Even after my fight with the captain?"

Cardosa jerked his chin toward Vinny, who sat alone in the corner. "You act like that guy doesn't do something stupid every week."

Oh great. It looked like Grant's fear of getting a reputation like "The Box" was coming true. He sighed. "Yeah."

"And yet everyone's happy when he's out there on game day because he's good at what he does." Cardosa gave Grant a hard look. "And so are you. Don't let one little argument get to you."

Grant nodded, but it wasn't just one little argument. Grant couldn't help but wonder if he'd messed things up with his dream girl for all the wrong reasons. Not that he could say that to Cardosa—or anyone, for that matter.

Thankfully, his little heart-to-heart with Cardosa was cut short when Coach stood up to give his pre-game pep-talk.

"This is our game. We're going to get the win tonight."

The guys all shouted in unison, though Grant's voice

was slightly less enthusiastic than usual.

"We're going to send Arizona back home with the L."

Cheers erupted all around him. The guys were hooting and hollering in response.

"Let's go get them."

One last cheer went through the locker room as they all filed out. The arena's lights were already dim, and spotlights flashed over the crowd. The guys bounced on the balls of their feet as they waited to be called.

As if he wasn't anxious enough, Coach had surprised him with a spot on the starting lineup for his first game back. Grant stood toward the back of the group as the announcer called the other players one by one. His heart raced knowing he would be out there soon doing the only thing that made sense anymore.

Finn stood directly behind him, and he could feel the captain's eyes boring into his back, but he refused to turn around. Grant had successfully ignored the captain during the warmup, other than the few times he'd taken a shot on goal. He had no desire to start talking to him now.

"On offense, number thirty-two, Silas Jenkins."

Silas ran out onto the field.

"On defense, number nine, Bastian Ramirez."

Bastian ran out onto the field.

"Playing midfield, number seven, Grant Vaughn."

Grant took a deep breath and plastered a smile on his face before he ran out onto the field. He waved at the stands as he made his way out to midfield.

He looked over at the seats next to the home bench—Em's seats—as the announcer called Finn's name. Frida and Miriam were cheering next to each other. His heart sank when he saw that Em was missing. He knew that he'd ended things, but he wanted to see her one last time.

Finn settled in a spot next to Grant. "She's not there," he said through gritted teeth as he smiled at the crowd.

Grant didn't want to have this talk right here, right now. He kept his fake smile plastered on his face. "I can see that."

The cheering quieted as students from a local elementary school walked out onto the field to sing the National Anthem. The players from both teams turned to face the flag and put their hands over their hearts.

Finn leaned in. His voice was low. "I don't know what happened while I was in Oregon—Frida and Em are being tight-lipped about it—but I have a feeling it involves you. I told you to stay away from her."

If going on a silly date as part of a halftime show earned him a black eye, he didn't want to know what would happen if he admitted he'd kissed her. Grant decided to answer in half-truths. "I told her that I couldn't date her."

Finn narrowed his eyes. "I don't believe you."

Grant lifted his shoulder. "Ask her."

Finn continued to stare at Grant as the kids finished singing. When they were done, and the players started walking to their spots, either on the field or on the bench, Finn reached out and grabbed Grant's arm.

Is he going to fight me moments before kickoff in front of all these fans?

"Don't think this conversation is over, *rookie*."

He shook Finn's hand off. "Of course not."

Apparently not dating Em, and then telling her that they shouldn't date, wasn't enough for Finn. Would things always be like that with the team's captain? If that was the case, maybe Grant should start applying to more master's programs outside of the state—and looking at other MASL teams too.

Grant jogged to his spot and looked at Em's seat once more. She still wasn't there, and he couldn't help but feel responsible for her missing something she enjoyed so much.

The ref blew his whistle, and the game began. Once the ball was in play, Grant pushed all thoughts of Em from his mind and focused on the game. He needed to walk the thin line of playing the best he could without pushing so hard he hurt himself again.

He could not imagine sitting out for another extended period of time.

Grant got to play for almost the entire first quarter, and by the time the buzzer rang, he'd had two assists—one to Silas and the other to Cardosa. Since Finn hadn't let any balls past, the team had a two-point lead.

It was a great way to make his comeback.

There was a short break—a chance for all the players to get water while the coaches discussed plays for the upcoming quarter. During this time, Greg, the GM, walked out to talk about one of the team's corporate sponsors.

Grant grabbed a towel to wipe the sweat from his face.

"You doing okay?" Coach asked.

This was the hardest he'd worked in a month, and his body was having a hard time adjusting, but it felt good to be part of the team. He nodded. "Yeah."

"He was getting slow at the end," Finn said. "It might be good to have him sit out the next quarter."

Grant bit his tongue. He wouldn't rise to the captain's bait. He could only hope that Coach would ignore Finn's advice and let Grant in anyway.

"Noted," Coach said before he started going into the plays he wanted the guys to try. The next couple minutes went by fast, and Grant soon found himself in the Storm's box watching his teammates play without him.

He'd successfully kept his eyes away from Em's seat during the first quarter, but now that he'd had a chance to catch his breath, his gaze went to where she should have been sitting.

She still wasn't there, but Frida happened to be looking toward the home bench and caught his eye. She gave him a sad smile and shook her head.

Needing to know more, Grant pushed his way to the end of the team's box and closer to Frida. When he got there, she refused to meet his gaze. Her entire body was stiff as she watched the game.

"Is she okay?"

"I shouldn't be talking to you, girl code and all."

"Shouldn't? Or won't?"

She let out a long sigh. "If Em sees me talking to you, she's not going to be happy with me, and I'm already on thin ice."

"How's she going to see us talking? She's not here." His breath caught in his chest. Em wasn't sitting in her usual spot. That didn't mean she wasn't in the arena. "She's here, isn't she?"

Frida bit her bottom lip.

"Where?"

"If I tell you, you can't look, okay?"

He snorted. Grant had been hoping to catch a glimpse of her all night. If Frida told him where Em was, he wouldn't be able to stop himself from looking in that direction.

Frida shifted on her feet. "Can you at least wait until you're not standing right next to me?"

"Fine. Where is she?"

Without taking her eyes off the game, she said, "Section two-twenty-five, about halfway up. Her hair is pulled back, and she's wearing a black tank top."

Grant fought to keep his head from turning in that section's direction. Frida had said she was on thin ice, and while Grant had no idea what had happened, he didn't want to make things worse for the two friends.

"Thank you," he said as he moved back to the other side, as far away from Frida as possible. Once there, his eyes went to section two-twenty-five, and he started looking frantically for Em.

It would be a lot easier to find you if your hair was down. But maybe that was the point. She'd gone through the effort of getting a ticket in a nosebleed section. Of course she wanted to remain anonymous.

That didn't stop him. He systematically went row by

row until he saw a girl sitting by herself. She wore a black tank top and her hair was in a ponytail, and even though he couldn't see her as well as he would have liked from his spot on the ground, he knew it was her.

She was here.

Grant hoped he would get one last chance to talk to her. He knew it was selfish, and he wasn't sure what he would say, but he was the moth and she was the flame. He couldn't stay away.

"Vaughn!"

Grant shook his head and looked toward the sound of the voice calling his name. Coach was looking at him with a frown. "Are you good to go back out?"

Knowing that Em was here, his body coursed with a new rush of adrenaline. "Absolutely."

"Good. I'm taking Barros out for a break, and I want you to take his spot."

Grant hopped over the board as Barros came back in through the small door that opened to the field. Once he was out there, he sprinted toward the ball and got possession. He drove it down the field toward the other team's goal, took a shot...goal!

The arena erupted into loud cheers, and his teammates all came running over to him. They took turns smacking his back, patting his head, and clapping. Even Finn's frown appeared less severe as he congratulated Grant on the goal.

But all of that meant nothing. He wanted to see Em cheer. Unfortunately, he'd lost her in the sea of fans.

EMMELINE

GRANT HAD SCORED after being on the field for less than a minute.

He'd run out there, stolen the ball from the other team, and made a goal. She wasn't as close to the field as usual, but from her spot high in the stands she'd seen the entire thing clearly—just like she'd seen him and Frida talking only moments before he'd been put in.

Did Frida think that if she kept her face turned toward the game, that Em wouldn't be able to see what was going on? Her best friend had talked to Grant for several minutes, and when he returned to his spot, his head had immediately turned to where she was sitting.

Well, he knows I'm here now. No sense in hiding in the nosebleeds anymore.

While everyone was standing and cheering for Grant's impressive goal, Em shuffled around other fans to the stairs. She walked down toward the box seats and pulled the ticket with her usual seat from her purse.

When she gave it to the guard manning the exclusive section, he put the wristband on her and let her pass.

She kept her eyes trained on Frida, and away from the players, and she found her spot. "Hey."

Frida's eyes widened before she pulled Em in for a hug. "You decided to come down after all."

Em squeezed her back. When she pulled away, she shook her head. "Well, since someone decided to rat me out."

Miriam, who had been standing there when Em first arrived, mumbled something about needing to set up the swag table and walked off.

Frida shrugged. "I couldn't help it. I know you said he broke things off and it's for the best, but he was acting so sad. He kept looking over here, and I know it wasn't for me—as pretty as I may be."

Em let out a small laugh at Frida's joke but immediately sobered. She could relate to Grant looking for her. She kept looking down at the home bench, and it wasn't for the rest of the players.

"Is there something you're not telling me?" Frida asked when Em didn't say anything.

"No, why?"

Frida's face scrunched up. "It's just he didn't act like a guy who didn't want to be with you. He looked like he was the one who had his heart broken."

"I didn't call things off, if that's what you're implying."

If Grant had wanted to make things official, she would have broken her stupid rule and done it gladly.

"He said he was going back to Kansas City when the season was over, and that he didn't want to do a long-distance thing."

Frida shook her head. "In a weird way, I understand why he did it."

Em shot her a look.

Frida lifted her hands. "I said I understood *why*, not that I was happy about it. I know you liked him—still like him. Maybe he regrets how things ended."

Em wasn't sure what to think about her best friend's musings. Maybe he regretted it, but that didn't change that it had happened. Grant had shown that he wasn't willing to put in the effort to have a relationship with her. He was just another guy who found her unworthy.

Why did she only fall for the terrible guys? She wasn't sure, but she didn't want to think about it anymore. It was too painful.

"I don't know, but I don't want to talk about Grant anymore. I came tonight to watch the game, support my brother, and that's it."

"Fair enough. I'll shut up unless one of our players scores," Frida said before turning her attention to the game.

WATCHING Grant out there was harder than Em realized it would be, and she was thankful for Frida's uncharacteristic strength. Her best friend didn't talk about Grant for the remainder of the game—even when he scored another goal. Frida cheered without nudging Em or wiggling her eyebrows or making jokes.

The final buzzer rang, and the Storm won the game with a three-point lead. Fans cheered as the players celebrated on the field. Another win meant they still got to enjoy their spot at the top of the Eastern Conference. If they could keep up the good work, they would get to go to the playoffs.

The Storm had never made it to the playoffs, and Em knew that Finn had to be excited, along with the rest of the team. It had to be especially exciting for Grant considering it was his first year playing.

Em allowed her eyes to search out Grant in the crowd in front of her. He was talking to other players, but his head turned toward her just as soon as her eyes landed on him—as if he knew she was looking at him.

Her breath caught in her chest when his blue eyes found hers. They didn't leave her face as he pushed his way through the other players and walked toward her. With every step closer, her heart beat faster until she thought it might beat right out of her chest when he stopped in front of her—only the waist-height board separating them.

"Hey."

Em crossed her arms to hide the trembling in her hands. "Hi."

"I, uh..." His eyes went to his feet.

"You played a great game tonight."

He looked up and gave her a sad smile. "Thanks."

"That goal was amazing."

His smile grew. "I was trying to impress a girl."

An ache filled her chest. "Don't say that. Not now."

He shook his head. "You're right. I just...how are you doing?"

How was she doing? Not great, and he was the last person she wanted to talk to about it. "Grant..."

"I'm sorry. I know this is tough. But I want you to know that I'm sorry for how things ended between us. I didn't want them to end, but I was already feeling stressed with my injury and the fact that I was breaking Finn's rule by talking to you." His eyes went wide. "What I mean is—"

"Finn's rule?" What was Grant talking about? Em had a rule. She'd made no secret of her rule when she talked to Grant. But this was the first time she'd heard of one from her brother.

Grant rubbed the back of his neck. "You should know that I always thought it was crap. But he made it abundantly clear that it wasn't up for debate."

Abundantly clear with his fist?

Grant had been quick to brush her off when she'd asked about his black eye last week. He hadn't wanted to say how he got it. Even now, Grant wasn't saying that Finn had hit him. But Em knew her brother well enough to know his preferred method of getting his way.

Or, at least, she thought she knew her brother. But since when did he lie to her about his relationships and set down edicts about her own? That wasn't the Finn she'd grown up with, and it made her question everything.

She put her hands on the board and leaned forward. "What's the rule, Grant?"

Grant's head briefly turned to where the players were standing and then back to Em. He lifted his hands to make air-quotes. "He has a strict 'no-dating-my-sister' rule."

"He what?" Her voice was high-pitched. "I have the no-dating-athletes rule."

Grant shrugged. "Well, he decided to take it one step further. No one on the team is allowed to even talk to you."

So that was why so many of the guys kept a safe distance when they talked to her. They didn't want a broken nose or a black eye. Though there was someone who got neither. "Do you know what happened with Damien?"

He shook his head and backed away. "Oh, no. That's something you'll have to ask Finn about."

Her hands clenched into fists. She was going to kill her brother for all the secrets he'd been keeping behind her back. "Anything else you think I should know?" she asked through clenched teeth.

He reached out like he wanted to touch her but let his hand drop to his side. "Just that I'm sorry that I hurt you. I never meant for things to end like that. I wish I could go back and have a do-over."

Grant's admission softened her anger, but it was quickly replaced with pain. She hadn't wanted things to end at all. She shook her head. "But we can't. What's done is done."

Grant's lips turned down into a frown.

The sight broke her heart. She turned her eyes away and saw the rest of the players were making their way off the field toward the locker rooms. Em jerked her head toward them. "You should probably get going."

Grant took a deep breath. "Yeah, okay."

Then he turned and walked off.

EM STAYED in the stands during the autograph session. She was too angry to pretend like everything was okay and knew if she tried to talk to Finn, she was going to lose it. Talking about how Finn had been scaring away guys was not a conversation she wanted to have in front of all of his teammates, though it sounded like they all knew about his stupid rule.

It was difficult to watch him smile and laugh with fans, and she was thankful when the crowd started to thin. When the last fan left the field, Finn looked around the arena. He spotted Em and waved.

She kept her face blank.

His brow crinkled, and he stood up. He said something to Silas and started walking toward her. When he made it up the stairs to where she sat, he smiled. "What are you doing way up here?"

Her eyes narrowed.

"What's going on? I thought you weren't mad about me dating Frida anymore."

"I'm not mad about that. I'm mad about the other secrets you've been keeping from me."

His brows lowered. "What are you talking about?"

"The little rule you have for all your teammates." She smiled tightly. "The one that says they're not allowed to date me."

He shifted on his feet.

"So, it's true. You've been telling guys to stay away from me."

"I—"

"Did you tell Grant to stay away?"

He nodded.

"Did you say it with your fist?"

He lowered his gaze.

She shook her head. "Why did you do that?"

He lifted his hands. "To protect you. I couldn't stand to see another guy hurt you. First Travis broke up with you. Then Mark did the same thing. I couldn't bear the thought of it happening again."

"People break up with other people all the time."

"Those people aren't my sister though."

She shook her head. "What about Damien? He wasn't exactly a great date, and I heard you had something to do with it."

He plopped down next to her and rubbed his hands over his face. "I didn't like the way some of the guys were looking at you—like you were a *woman*. Even after I broke Parrera's nose, there were a few that didn't care. So I told Damien to take you out and show you a bad time. I figured it would push you over the edge and you'd stop dating athletes altogether. Then I wouldn't have to work so hard to keep the guys away."

"Unbelievable."

"It worked, didn't it?"

She crossed her arms and lifted her chin. "You had no right."

"What was I supposed to do, Em? Sit back and watch you get hurt over and over again?"

"Yes, that's exactly what you were supposed to do."

His eyebrows shot up.

"I don't like the idea of getting hurt any more than you do, but you're not the keeper of my heart, Finn. You're my brother, the one man I thought I could trust."

How many relationships did she miss out on because Finn had scared guys away? And how many had she pushed away because she'd been so easily manipulated by her brother into thinking that a no-athlete rule was a good idea?

Guys like Grant.

She'd enjoyed talking to him from that first day at City Bar and had pushed him away until he finally left for good. Tears streamed down her cheeks.

Finn reached out and rubbed her arm. "I'm sorry."

Em turned in her seat. "You can't keep secrets from me anymore."

"I know."

"I'm serious, Finn. You are the only family I have, and I need to know that I can trust you. Let me make my own mistakes instead of trying to protect me."

"I only want what's best for you." Finn wrapped his arm around Em and pulled her close. "From now on, I promise. No more secrets."

"You'll let me make my own mistakes," she said. "But you can give me advice on how to handle jerks on my own without beating them up."

He considered it for a moment. Eventually, he nodded. "Deal."

Em rested her head on his shoulder. "Thank you."

They sat in uncomfortable silence for several minutes, both looking down at the empty arena below them.

Finn was the first to speak. "So, does this mean you like Grant?"

Em sat up. Her first reaction was to brush off Finn's question. They didn't talk about relationships other than when boys had hurt her. Maybe that was part of the problem. If they had talked about the good things in addition to the bad—if they had had uncomfortable conversations like this—then maybe Finn wouldn't have decided to scare away guys.

Maybe Em would have never made her stupid rule in the first place.

She took a deep breath. "Yeah. I really like him." She paused. "Or, *liked* him, I guess. Things are most definitely over at this point."

"Are you sure?"

She bit her bottom lip. "Pretty sure."

"Because of me."

She snorted. "I'm sure you punching him had something to do with it. But that wasn't all of it."

"Have you tried talking to him? I hear you're getting really good at heart-to-hearts."

Em laughed. She'd made up with her best friend and her brother in the past week even though it had meant having conversations that put her way out of her comfort zone. But she was still far from being good at heart-to-hearts. Besides, there were too many other variables to consider. Grant was the one to walk away. Not only that, he'd be going back to Kansas City when the season was over.

She shook her head. "I think this one might be beyond repair.

21

GRANT

THEY'D JUST FINISHED practice when Finn stormed over to where Grant was gathering his things. "We need to talk."

Grant sighed loudly. *Oh great. What did I do this time?*

He hadn't spoken to Em since last week's game, and while he knew that he shouldn't have even done that, she looked so sad and beautiful standing there he couldn't resist going to her.

Grant was just surprised it took Finn so long to dish out the consequences. He looked to see if anyone else still lingered in the arena, but they'd all left pretty quickly.

How convenient.

He braced himself for the verbal—and possibly physical—attack.

He closed his eyes. "Why don't you just punch me and get it over with?"

"I'm not here to fight with you."

With everything that had happened this past week, Grant didn't have any patience left. He looked at Finn. "Then what? Are you here to tell me to quit playing for the Storm? Do you want me to refuse the offer to play here again next year?"

Finn wouldn't be happy until Grant was out of the picture completely. It was the reason his Storm contract for next year's season lay unsigned—right next to an unopened letter from USF.

Grant knew he shouldn't stay; he needed to go back home to Kansas City and forget all about the life he was building in Waterfront. He couldn't though. Every time he tried to rip up the contract or throw away the envelope that contained an answer from USF about the master's program, he stopped himself at the last moment.

He didn't want to leave the Storm. And he sure as hell didn't want to leave Em.

Finn's brows lowered. "Greg already offered you a place next year?"

"Yeah. But I haven't signed it yet, so don't worry. You can still bully me into leaving," he said in a sharp tone.

Finn took a deep breath and pinched the bridge of his nose. "I just wanted to talk for a minute. Can you give me that? Please?"

Grant just about fell over in shock. Did Finn, the same guy who'd given him a black eye just a couple weeks ago, just say *please*? "Uh, okay."

"It's about Emmeline."

Emmeline?

He couldn't think of any reason for Finn to talk about

his sister...unless something was wrong. His entire body tensed. "Is she okay?"

"She's fine, but she's been really upset. Someone told her about my rule."

Grant kept his lips closed. He still wasn't sure if he should expect a fist coming at his face, and he didn't want to push it by saying something stupid.

Finn ran a hand through his hair. "For some reason, Em likes you, and I've realized she gets to decide who she wants to date."

Too bad Finn couldn't have had this epiphany a few weeks ago—before Grant had called things off with her. "That ship has already sailed."

"Does that mean you don't like her?"

"I really like her, more than any other woman I've ever dated. She's smart, funny, kind, and *gorgeous*."

Finn cleared his throat. "And still my little sister."

"Right." Grant nodded, glad that he didn't mention how amazing their kiss was now that Finn was looking at him with his intimidating game face. "Ending things with her was one of the hardest things I've ever done."

Finn adjusted his stance. "Then why did you do it?"

"I did it because I like her so much. I was planning to go back to Kansas City when the season was over. I didn't want to hurt her by dragging things out. That wouldn't be fair to her."

Finn narrowed his eyes. "*Was* planning? Does that mean you're staying?"

His response suddenly felt important, but Grant still

wasn't sure if he planned to stay or not. He shrugged. "I don't know."

Finn made a *hmm* sound. "You said Greg already offered you a spot next season, right?"

Grant nodded.

"Then what's the hang-up?"

"Your sister. *She's* the hang-up." Grant threw his arms out. "Seeing her after the game the other night was really hard. It would be impossible to keep playing here knowing that she would be watching from those box seats—to know I couldn't talk to her afterward."

Finn's eyes were unfocused as they looked off to the side. "Believe it or not, I get that." He closed his eyes for a moment and looked back at Grant. "But let's say she wanted to be with you, would you stay?"

"But she doesn't."

Finn cocked his head. "Humor me."

Grant hated the way his pulse picked up at the mere thought of Em wanting to be with him. He knew it wasn't the case…but what if it was? Grant would sign next year's contract for the Storm tomorrow and start looking for a place in Waterfront as soon as possible. "Of course I would."

"Then I want to help you get her back."

Grant lowered his brows. "I don't understand."

Finn reached out and squeezed his shoulder. "I made some mistakes that I'm trying to fix.

"And that somehow involves playing matchmaker with me and your sister?"

"For now, it does. But if you ever hurt—"

"I would never hurt her. Not again."

Finn stared at him for a moment as if he were trying to determine if Grant was telling the truth. "Good. Then we both have the same goal—happy Em. Now we just need to figure out how to make it happen."

Grant wasn't sure if Finn had a plan, or if it would work. But as the possibility of fixing things with Em took hold, Grant realized he would do whatever it took—even if that meant he would have to work with Finn.

22

EMMELINE

EM WAS JUST STEPPING out of the shower when she heard her phone buzzing from the bathroom counter. She quickly wrapped a towel around herself and looked at the screen. The name on the screen surprised her.

Why is Miriam calling me?

While Em and the team's community outreach coordinator enjoyed spending time together during games, she'd never called her for anything. Especially not on a Saturday morning.

What was going on?

She swiped the screen and held her phone to her ear. "Hello?"

Miriam's words came out in a rush. "Oh, thank goodness you answered. I've called you three times in the last ten minutes."

Her heart raced in her chest. "What's wrong?"

"What are you doing right now?"

She walked out of the bathroom and sat on the edge

of her bed. "I've been cleaning my apartment all morning and just took a shower. Why?"

"How fast can you come down to the arena?"

Tonight's game wasn't for several more hours. A sinking feeling of dread settled in her belly. "Did something happen to Finn?" She paused. "To Grant?"

"What? No. They're fine," Miriam said. "But I really need your help with something."

Em let out a sigh, but her relief was short-lived and soon replaced with irritation. "Why did you scare me like that? I thought something was wrong."

"Oh, something *is* wrong. I've been working on another Storm project and nothing is coming together how I wanted it to. I was hoping you could help me."

Miriam had gotten Em all worked up over a Storm project? Em shook her head. "I don't know," she said.

"Please, Em. I know it's last minute, but I'll owe you one."

Em laughed. "I'm pretty sure you said that last time. And it's not just because it's last minute." The last time she'd agreed to help Miriam, Em had ended up on *The Dating Game*, and that had ended in disaster.

"Fine." She huffed. "I'll owe you two. Three. A hundred. Whatever you want. I just really need your help."

Em couldn't believe she was actually going to say yes. She ran her fingers through her wet hair. "Yeah. Okay. Let me get dressed really quick, and I'll head down."

"You can, uh, spend a little time on yourself first. Dry your hair, do your makeup...maybe wear a dress."

Why would she have to do her hair and makeup? Or wear a dress? "What kind of project is this?"

"You'll see when you get here."

"Miriam."

"I promise you'll like it. Just make sure you actually come, okay?"

"Okay," she said, still confused.

Warning bells went off in her head, but Em had already agreed. And if she was being honest with herself, part of her was curious about what Miriam was cooking up.

Not sure of what to expect, she took the extra time to do her hair and makeup, and headed down to the arena.

EM ARRIVED an hour later and walked through the empty halls of the civic center. When she opened the doors that led to the arena, Miriam was already standing there waiting for her.

I hope she hasn't been here since we hung up.

Miriam's mouth broke out into a wide grin, and she pulled Em in for a hug. "I'm so glad you came."

"I told you I would," Em said, pulling away.

"Which is good. Can you go check on something I left on the field?"

Em's brows lowered. "Uh, sure. What is it?"

"Don't worry, you'll know it when you see it."

"Do you need me to do anything with it?"

"No, you don't have to do anything." Miriam giggled.

"Just go make sure everything is okay in there, and I'll be right back."

"O-kay." Em shook her head as she walked into the stands. The lights were off, and she wasn't sure how she was supposed to find what Miriam left in there when it was so dark. The only light in the entire room was a soft glow that came from midfield. When Em looked more closely, she saw the light was coming from a table covered in candles—and someone was standing beside it.

Grant.

He was the thing Miriam left on the field?

Breathless, she carefully walked toward the table. She was glad that she'd listened to Miriam and dressed up since Grant was wearing a suit. The urge to play with the curls she'd put in her hair or smooth her hands over her dress was hard to fight under his watchful gaze, but she did not want him to see the effect he had on her even now. She held her head high as she got closer.

"Wow," he breathed when she stopped in front of him. "You look gorgeous."

Em's cheeks heated. She looked down at her feet in hopes of hiding her reaction to his words. "Thank you."

"I'm glad you came."

She looked back up, keeping her features blank. "Miriam said she needed help with something. If I'd known that this was her project, I might not have shown up." The words and her tone sounded harsh to her ears, but she didn't apologize for either. Grant had hurt her—deeply—and now he was trying to...what? Em still didn't know. "What is this?"

"This is me trying to apologize." Grant sighed loudly and shook his head.

It was the most elaborate apology she'd ever gotten. Decorating the field on game day was risky. "Does Coach know you're making a mess of his field so close to kickoff?"

"Since he hasn't stormed the field yet, I can only assume the answer is no."

"And how exactly did you pull this off without him knowing?"

"With a lot of help from Miriam...and your brother."

Finn had helped Grant with this? Now she really was shocked. But she still wasn't sure what Grant was hoping to accomplish with a table and some candles. "Why?"

His brows lowered. "Why what?"

She put her hands out. "Why did you do all this? The suit, the table, the candles?"

"I was hoping I could take you on a proper date."

A date?

Even though Em could appreciate the effort he'd gone through, did he really think he could light some candles and everything would be fine? Things weren't fine. She shook her head. "You and I both know this isn't going to work out. You said yourself that you're going back to Kansas City when the season is over. And just like you, I don't want to have a long-distance relationship. Going down this road will only lead to more heartache."

"What if I wasn't leaving?"

Her brows lowered. "What are you talking about?"

"Please just sit with me for a little while and I'll explain."

Speechless, she nodded.

Grant walked around the table and pulled out a chair for Em. When she was comfortable, he walked around to his side and sat down. He pulled a bottle of champagne and two glasses. "Would you like a drink?"

"Yes, please," she said, though it was going to take more than a glass of champagne to settle her nerves.

Grant opened the bottle and poured the bubbly liquid into both of their glasses.

"So, you're staying in Waterfront?"

Grant opened his suit jacket and pulled out an envelope from the inside pocket. He slid it across the table. "I recently applied to a couple masters programs. One of them was USF."

Her eyes went to the envelope on the table. She wanted to know when he applied—and why. Was it too much to hope that she had something to do with his decision? She took a shaky breath. "Why are you telling me all this?"

"I didn't want to end things. I've regretted it every day since I let you walk out my door. I figured if I got into a local school, I would have an excuse to stay. And if I stayed, I might get another chance." He reached out and grabbed her hand.

So she *had* been a factor in applying to a Florida school, and now he was asking for another chance. Warmth filled her chest. She wanted to say yes, but there was a small voice in the back of her mind warning her that she'd only get hurt again. The idea of facing another rejection from Grant was unbearable. She pulled her hand away and picked up the envelope. "When do you start?"

He rubbed the back of his neck. "I don't actually know if I got accepted yet."

"I don't understand."

He shrugged. "I haven't opened it."

What was wrong with him? Why go through all the trouble of applying only to not open the envelope? "Why not?"

"I wasn't sure what I would do if they didn't accept me." He shook his head. "Or what I would do if they did."

"Then how can you sit there across from me and say you want another chance when you don't even know if you're going to stay?"

Without asking for permission, she grabbed the envelope off the table and tore the edge. She stared at him as she pulled the letter out, daring him to stop her. He didn't.

Em unfolded the paper and read the first line.

Congratulations. You've been accepted into the master's program at the University of South Florida's School of Business.

He got in. This was great news.

Or was it?

It was one thing for Grant to stay in Florida if he were to go to school at USF—he'd already said that he would. But would he still feel so passionate about another chance with Em if he wasn't accepted into the program? She needed to know how much he wanted to be with her.

She turned her lips down into a frown. "I'm so sorry. You didn't get in."

His shoulders slumped. "I have to say, I imagined this going differently. I really thought I would get accepted."

"It's okay. You can always apply for a school back home."

He shook his head. "No, I don't want to go back to Kansas City. I still want to stay here. I'll just have to figure out another plan. I can try online programs, put it on hold or something, but I'm not leaving Waterfront."

Hope built in Em's chest. "You aren't?"

He leaned forward and looked her in the eye. "I'm serious when I say that I want another chance with you Em. What we have is special, and I'm not going to let silly rules or rejection letters get in the way of that."

He wanted her—not because it was convenient or easy, but because of who she was. He'd hurt her, but she was willing to give him another chance because she wanted him too.

"Good answer," she said with a small smile. "Because you got into the program."

His brows lowered.

Em turned the letter around. "This is an acceptance letter."

He snatched the paper out of her hands. His lips spread into a wide grin as he scanned the page. "But you said…"

"I wanted to know how serious you were about staying here. I needed to know it was more than a whim."

Grant stood up and walked over to where Em sat. He grabbed her hand and gently pulled her up so that they were both standing. His hand reached out, and his fingers ran over her cheek. "You're more than a whim. You are the most amazing woman I've ever met, and somewhere along the way, I fell in love with you."

Grant *loved* her?

Her heart felt like it would burst with his words.

She wrapped her arms around the back of Grant's neck and lifted up on her toes so that her face was even with his. Dizzy with the desire to be near him, she pulled him closer so that their lips were almost touching.

He smiled, causing small crinkles in the corners of his eyes. "Does this mean you feel the same way?"

Yes. She absolutely felt the same way.

Even though she hadn't named the feelings she had for him before this moment, she now knew that she felt the same. It was why it hurt so much when he'd said they couldn't be together. She loved Grant. The thought rendered her speechless for the second time that night. Thankfully, she didn't need words to tell him how she felt.

Em closed the small distance between their lips and kissed him with the unspoken words from the last few weeks. She hoped that he could feel the emotions in what she couldn't say aloud. She was foolish to push him away for so long. She loved him. She never wanted him to go.

By the way he moved his lips against hers, he could

hear her loud and clear. She tightened her grip on him as his hands slid down her arms and around her waist.

They were finally on the same page about what they wanted, and that was each other. Now that they finally realized this, nothing was going to stand in their way—not even a silly rule.

23

EMMELINE

EM'S LIPS still tingled as the announcer called the players out to the field one-by-one for that night's game.

She wasn't sure how long she and Grant had been kissing before Miriam had come out onto the field and told them they needed to break it up and clean up the evidence of their date before the civic center started allowing fans to enter the arena.

Even the embarrassment of having Miriam walk in on them making out wasn't enough to make her want to stop. Their time on the field hadn't felt like nearly enough.

It would never be enough.

Now that she'd officially thrown herself into a relationship with Grant, she didn't want to spend a minute apart. There was too much lost time to make up for, and if Em had her way, much of that time would be spent kissing.

For now, she'd have to settle for fangirling over him from the sidelines.

"On defense, number seventy-seven, Vinny Nelson."

Assuming the announcer ever called him out. Em clapped her hands for Vinny as he made his way out to midfield.

"Team captain and keeper, number one, Finn O'Brien!"

Em cheered but kept her eyes on her hands as her brother ran out. Even though he'd helped Grant with the secret date, she was afraid that he would take one look at her and know just how that date was spent. He might be okay with Grant and Em dating, but that might be too much too fast.

"Number seven, Grant Vaughn."

Em's heart raced as Grant came into view. When his eyes met hers, her cheeks flamed.

Miriam jabbed her in the ribs with her elbow. "Are you still going to pretend like you don't have a crush on him?"

"I don't."

Miriam laughed. "You don't have to lie about it."

"I'm not lying," she said, her eyes still fixed on Grant. He looked so handsome standing out there. She wanted to jump over the boards and rush to him. She smiled wide at Miriam. "It's not a crush. It's much more than that."

ACKNOWLEDGMENTS

God first, always.

Then my husband.

Then my kids.

J & A, I don't know what I'd do without you guys. Thanks for putting up with me.

Elle, once again, you're a saint!

And so are you, Angela! Thanks for your help!

To the Tropics players who keep answering all my questions (Rob and JP especially), thank you!

And, last but never least, to all the readers who have kept this dream alive for three years: thank you for reading my books. All of this would be impossible without you.

ABOUT KAYLA

Kayla has loved to read as long as she can remember. While she started out reading spooky stories that had her hiding under her covers, she now prefers stories with a bit more kissing.

When she gets a chance to watch TV, she enjoys cheesy sci-fi and superhero shows. Most days, you'll catch her burning dinner in an attempt to cook while reading just one more chapter.

Find me online:
www.tirrellblewrites.com

ALSO BY KAYLA TIRRELL

Varsity Girlfriends:

Courtside Crush

Game Plan

Wedding Games:

The Bridesmaid & The Reality Show

The Bridesmaid & The Ex

The Bridesmaid & Her Surprise Love

Love in the Arena:

Penalty Box

Out of Play

River Valley Lost & Found:

All The Things We Lost

All The Things We Found

All The Things We Were

Disastrous Dates:

Disastrous Dates: A Sweet College Romance

Made in United States
Orlando, FL
14 March 2025